THE COMEBACK CATCHER

Books by T. Morris Longstreth

Henry Thoreau: American Rebel

The Comeback Catcher

The Comeback Catcher

By T. MORRIS LONGSTRETH

DODD, MEAD & COMPANY, NEW YORK

To my baseball-playing friends
Buzz Burger, catcher,
&
Greg Frazier, pitcher,
who helped

Library of Congress Catalog Card Number: 65-20909
Printed in the United States of America
by The Cornwall Press, Inc., Cornwall, N. Y.

Contents

1. DOWN, OUT, AND LICKED • 1

2. WOE VS. WILL • 15

3. PART OF AN IDEA • 23

4. WINDFALL WEEK • 30

5. HOW TO BUILD A BALL TEAM • 41

6. HOW TO KILL A BALL TEAM • 49

7. JAMES ANTAEUS MCNAIL • 62

8. THE BATTLE OF PEBBLE CREEK • 69

9. THREE-RING JAMES • 79

10. ON THE LAKE • 92

11. AN OBSTACLE RACE MONTHS LONG • 96

12. THE BLOW FALLS • 115

13. "WHAT DO YOU WANT TO KNOW?" • 120

14. BRIEF INTERLUDE • 133

15. ON THE WAY • 138

16. "WHOEVER SAW A YES-CAT?" • 146

17. CLIFF-HANGING AT CLIFFSIDE • 153

18. *THE* GAME • 160

19. THE WINNING LOSS • 179

1

Down, Out, and Licked

JIM MC NAIL, aged seventeen, the long-boned son of a Pennsylvania farmer, was as busy that May afternoon as three beavers at a dam-break.

He was manning the McNail farm's roadside fruit and vegetable stand. Customers, like radishes, came in bunches, and three parties were lined up along the counter, asking prices, probing the heads of lettuce, and producing five-dollar bills for a thirty-cent purchase.

Meanwhile, exciting news issued from the radio beside the cash register. The Phillies were 2 to St. Louis' 0 in the second inning. But each time Philadelphia ran the count up to some critical point, a customer called Jim from the game. Worse than that, his sister Jean had promised to relieve him at two o'clock, in time for him to watch Ironwood School's baseball team play against Cliffside. It was now nearly three, and Jim would gladly have handed his dear sister, aged a flighty fifteen, over to the cannibals. What could she be doing? Reading, no doubt—but this time, she had promised positively not to be late.

Abruptly, the customers left, like startled crows with thefts on their conscience, and Jim turned up the radio. The third inning was half over, and the score still remained 2 to 0. The bases, Jim thrilled to hear, were fully occupied by the home team, but, just as the St. Louis pitcher threw, the announcer was interrupted by another voice saying, "Unfortunately, we must interrupt . . ."

Jim muttered some highly uncomplimentary phrases. Who wanted to hear about some other remote emergency when the Phillies' catcher had a chance to bring in three runs? He felt a special bond with catchers, being one himself.

Jim called Bogie, his Irish retriever, to him and told him what to do if he ever met a news announcer. The dog wiggled his brief tail, plus his rear, in total agreement. Bogie was a yes-dog when Jim commanded. Scott McNail, a year younger than Jim, complained that Bogie's brain was the size of an undeveloped lima bean. Even that put the retriever ahead of Scott, was Jim's retort. The two brothers were very good for each other. Thanks to ceaseless inspection, neither allowed the head of the other to enlarge unduly. Yet, underneath the verbal dueling lay mutual affection and even respect, and each boy would have fought Ironwood Village singlehanded had the other been maligned.

As the announcer polished off the weather, which was clear, cloudless, windless, a perfect day for baseball, Jim's temper was subjected to a new strain. A shiny limousine stopped near the stand and a well-padded woman rolled out of the rear seat and waddled over to the strawberries which Jim had picked that morning, after finishing the milking. Any boy who can run a ball team from behind the plate knows how to use his eyes, and Jim could tell from the way the customer inspected each individual strawberry that this sale would take ages. "Are you sure these berries are fresh?" she asked.

"No, they're last year's," he wanted to say, but he curbed his response to a mere, "Yes, ma'am."

"How about the lettuce?" The woman felt the dewy green heads.

Had this exasperating customer bothered to look at Jim, she would have seen something remarkable–strength in control of itself. The young man was tall, fair, apparently intelligent, but the set of his long jawbone, rather angular chin, and firmly held mouth gave a hint of his power over himself. The sharp light in his blue eyes should have scared her a little, but her attention had turned to the carrots. She picked up a bunch and counted them.

Fortunately for the corked volcano, just then a girl came loping down the maple-shaded McNail lane, carrying a book. Jean McNail was also fair and slightly freckled. Her perpetual zest for life came from being undilutedly herself. Just as Jim's inmost virtue was tenacity, which brother Scott described as the stubbornness of mules, so Jean's central gift was grace of spirit. She loved. It showed in her face so clearly that, even in the heat of Jim's ire, he could not bear to demolish her, especially before this strange woman.

"I'm so sorry, Jim. Really I am. It was Marybelle–"

"In Boston, I suppose, for half an hour?"

Jean nodded. "I tried to remind her, but it was so important. Larry had taken her to such a thrilling show . . ."

Jim's wrath faded for, like other masculine beings of his age, he could not hang on to bad temper when girls were concerned, even with his own sister. And Jean was temper-proof. She also was always so extremely sorry at failing him that she would have disarmed a man-eating tiger. Jim was not a tiger. He was a baseball enthusiast in a hurry to watch Ironwood whip Cliffside, so he promptly turned over to Jean the lingering customer, who was now pawing over the string beans. "The new list of prices is by the register," he told her. "Make up the customer's mind for her. She's good for ten bucks."

"I will, I will," Jean whispered. "I hope Ironwood wins twelve to nothing."

"Two to one would suit me. Cliffside's strong this year." Jim ran to his car, which was an extraordinary combination of previous vehicles. Bogie jumped from under its shade as if he slept on springs. Jim held open the door of what might have been termed a Ford, for the Ford strain predominated. Jim had bought the chassis from Ernie's Car Emporium in Ironwood Village for seven bucks. It had lacked wheels, radiator, carburetor, and the trunk was dented in. Jim had then dug up some wheels from a junk heap and squeezed a radiator out of Ernie for four dollars. The owner of the Emporium had thrown in some overworked tires. After collecting other odds and ends associated with a car, Jim figured triumphantly that his transportation would cost something like .00005 mill per mile!

He now urged the contraption to its upper speed, with Bogie the picture of satisfaction beside him. To be with Jim anywhere was joy, but to be in a car with him was bliss equal, almost, to chasing rats on the Burnsbrook Farm premises.

They curved around the outlet of Ironwood Lake, then climbed uphill to the cluster of handsome buildings and playing fields that comprised the century-old Ironwood School. Jim edged his car in between a Cadillac and an imported Triumph. Bogie started to follow his pal out of the car but Jim said, "No, stay with it, boy." The dog gave one heartbreaking look at his master—and obeyed. "Good boy!" Jim praised and, because he knew the ways of certain youth with inviting property, he added, "Keep your eye on 'em, fellow." Then he ran.

Muffled cheers from the battlefield puzzled Jim. They did not sound as if Ironwood were enjoying a victorious afternoon. He headed for the wire screen back of the plate. Watching from there was next best to standing in the umpire's shoes. He noticed that Ironwood was at bat. Then the scoreboard stabbed him—twice: Cliffside was ahead 5 to 2, and the game was already in the last half of the fifth inning. He was angry all over again at having missed so much, and bruised by the score. But he had to muzzle his feelings because, to his surprise, a lone girl was occupying his favored spot, her forehead pressed against the wire netting in her concentration. She had not even bothered to turn her head at the sound of his hurried approach.

This was all right with Jim. He was warmly hospitable to girls, but not on the ball field. At any other time and place, this one would have detained his experienced attention. He could not help noticing that she was almost a head shorter than six foot one. Her dark hair framed her face in the prevailing fashion. A second glance at the board showed him that Cliffside had scored all five runs in the first inning, while Ironwood had picked up one run in the third and one in the fourth. That offered hope. "How many down?" he asked impersonally, as if his neighbor had been a bat kid.

The girl looked at Jim for the first time, and then kept on looking for that extra half-second to which he was accustomed. "Two," she answered.

"And it's full count for Plinky Downs— Oh, boy!"

The sharp crack of bat on ball set Plinky deer-running, but a roar from the visitors' cheering section split the May breeze as the Cliffside right fielder nailed the ball. The nine in the neat buff uniform headed for their benches.

"Not once! Not once do we get a break!" the girl wailed. "All afternoon the same."

Jim noticed that Ironwood's substitute pitcher was heading for the mound. "Why Bailey?" he asked. "Did Everson crack?"

This time the girl glanced at him as one of the family. "No, he was hit on the left arm by the first Cliffside batter up. Ted's a southpaw, you know. He'd thrown a fast one and it came back faster. Coach Parsons sent MacQuarrie in, and Cliffside got five in a row before Parsons sent in Bailey. He's held them ever since. But we've had only five hits and all wasted."

"The game's seven innings, as usual?"

"Oh, yes!" the girl exclaimed indignantly. "As if schools were kindergartens! These boys will be college men in four months. Two more innings wouldn't kill them."

Jim agreed. He found himself agreeing in lots of ways with this feminine ball addict and hoped she wasn't a senior, about to graduate. This time next year, if his plan worked out, he'd be catching for Ironwood. He had a fleeting mental picture of managing the team from home plate with this girl standing behind the screen—approving. Bad luck wouldn't have a show. Jim scorned that excuse, anyway. His father had trained him to look for causes instead of fooling himself with a bad-luck story. That last put-out hadn't been bad luck, but the right fielder's skill. If Ted Everson's arm had got in the way of the ball, it was his lack of skill.

Bailey was throwing curves without much stuff on them, Jim saw. But Cliffside was tired or overconfident or just plain careless. Their first batter up hit too close to third base and good fielding nailed him to first base. The next Cliffsider fouled for an easy catch. The next batter shoved a grounder left of shortstop and reached the bag. Two on and Jim went taut.

"Watch this batter," the girl said. "He's dangerous."

Jim knew the Ironwood signals and, while he could not see the details, he gathered that the catcher was telling Bailey to give the batter one low, fast, and inside. Bailey tried, but the ball sped fatly down the middle. The Cliffsider slammed a low line sizzler between second and third, and the shortstop, intercepting with a clean catch, tossed to third in time to anticipate the runner. It was a sharp double play and the Ironwood stand roared approval.

"That changes things," the girl said.

But not for long. The first Ironwood batter looped a single to left field, but no clean-up hitter followed. The second batter hooked a low fast ball to the third baseman's mitt. The last batter fanned.

The Cliffsiders died of overconfidence or inertia in their last time at bat. Bailey wasted nothing and got the side out in a dozen pitches.

"That's the best inning of the season!" the girl exclaimed. "Now we need only four runs! We'd get them, too, if Ted could play! He's best in a pinch. He has really won three of our games this season by coming up from behind."

"I know. He's got the big swing that's the sign of a long-ball hitter."

"Have you been coming to the games regularly?"

"Since I could walk," Jim answered quietly.

Something in his low, well-rounded voice held the girl's attention. But the Ironwood batter stopped further talk by hitting a tremendous ball that started the left fielder running backwards, then turning and racing at frantic speed.

"He's wasting his time," the girl said triumphantly. "That ball's headed for the Pocono Mountains. Good old Severance! His last play before graduating. But there's our hard luck again, a home run and nobody on!"

Cliffside took the hint, closed ranks, struck out the first and second Ironwooder and caught the final player's foul. The customary yells were given, the crowd began to unravel and drift away. The girl's quick hopes at the home run had melted into near tears. Jim was glad to see that she took it hard, too. It made them two of a kind. He believed in caring desperately, with all one's being. But he was sensible enough to close out a proven loss without wasting time and energy on regrets. He reminded the girl that Ironwood had had a good season: seven victories to two defeats.

"Yes, but this walk-over ruins everything. Cliffside will gloat for a year."

"It's been three years since that school took the game."

"You do follow us!" the girl exclaimed. "Do you live across the lake?"

"Yes, but not in Ironwood Village. Four miles beyond, on the Burnsbrook Road. That was named for my grandfather's farm and we're still farmers."

"Lucky you!" the girl exclaimed and radiance came back into her face. "We live at the top of an elevator shaft in Philadelphia, fifteen floors up. But you ought to be here if you love Ironwood so much."

Jim's Scottish blood and pride made it hard for him to mention scarcity of money in his family. The girl, who was quick to understand his silence, said, "Ironwood gives many scholarships, you know. I'm here on one."

This confession warmed Jim all over. It brought him instantly nearer to her. Ironwood Village was accustomed to suppose that the gay-sounding students at the exclusive school on the hill across the lake were all rich. To his surprise, Jim, who was rarely impulsive, heard himself say, "I plan to come here next year."

Before this, he had not allowed himself to reveal this dream of his to anyone. It was his biggest secret, his life's demanding ambition. He grew hot with embarrassment at giving himself away like a blab-mouth to this stranger, yet there was an air of sympathetic interest about her that encouraged confidences.

She was searching his face as she asked, "But wouldn't you be a senior? You look older than most of our seniors?"

"I'm sixteen," he conceded. "I'm a senior at Ironwood Village School and get mostly B's. But your standards are so much higher, it would pay me to take the year over. I could try for one of those National Merit scholarships."

Something he had said was wrong, although he could not imagine what it was. "Have you asked Master Paul Atwood?" she questioned. "He's our dean of admissions."

"I've been waiting until school was over and my grades are in. It isn't too late, is it?"

"Perhaps not," She hesitated. "I don't think they accept anyone for just one year, though."

"What's wrong with that?" Jim's momentary chill of apprehension fled before his combativeness. Ever since his childhood, he had faced up to balks, and most of them had yielded to his determination. His friends called him strong-willed, the others called him stubborn.

The girl was sorry for the disappointment she had caused and said, "Mr. Ironwood may make an exception in your case, as you are a local boy. He does everything he can for the Village."

They were interrupted by the arrival of Ted Everson. The girl started to commiserate but he broke in with, "We can chew that over when I'm dressed, Laurie. See you outside the library in twenty minutes." Jim felt a chilled outsider, for the Ironwood pitcher had ignored his presence.

Laurie asked Ted, "Do you know whether students are ever accepted for the senior year only?"

"Sure. You mean your brother's changed his mind about not coming here?"

"No, Dick wouldn't—even if he had one."

Ted said, "There was that German boy, remember? And the Negro boy from Florida."

"That's so; I forgot." Laurie turned to Jim as Ted loped off. "Why don't you see Master Paul Atwood today? He's a prince. I know he'll do everything he can—I mean about scholarship aid. I can show you where he lives."

Jim glanced down at his jeans, which were clean—but jeans. Laurie read his mind and said, "You look all right. Who cares at a ball game? I believe in doing things now."

"So do I," Jim concurred. He and this girl certainly thought alike in more things than baseball. . . . They had just reached the school lane when they were hailed by a lanky, middle-aged man who was being pulled along by a small boy, tugging at his hand.

"Oh, Master Paul," Laurie said, "I was looking for you. May we bother you for a moment? Here's a future Ironwooder—we hope." Jim warmed at her friendly "*we* hope."

"The Dean of Admissions eyed Jim's athletic length of limb and open face with its good strong jaw in brief appraisal as he said to Laurie, "You couldn't bother me if you tried." Then he held out a hand to the boy, who introduced himself.

Laurie said "Good luck" to Jim, and to Dean Atwood, "I mustn't keep Ted waiting," and left.

The Dean turned to Jim, "What can I do for a future Ironwooder—*I* hope."

"Make me one now," Jim answered. Ever since I could hold a baseball, I've wanted to play for Ironwood. I've saved nearly eight hundred dollars to come here as a day student. I know it costs more, but if you can make me a scholarship loan, I could pay it back in a few years."

The smile faded from the Dean's face. "If it were only money, there'd be no trouble at all, Jim. But you're past your junior year, aren't you?"

"I'm finishing my senior year this June. But there's any amount that Ironwood can give me. . . ."

"Here's the situation, Jim," the older man said kindly. "We try to take nobody for a single year—especially the senior year. We feel that our very busy school staff cannot devote the special time and care required to adjust a boy in so many ways when he will not be here long enough to become a true part of the student body in its spirit."

Jim's fighting nature, always just under the surface, prompted him to reply, "But you did take on the German boy for one year, and the Negro from Florida."

Dean Atwood, who admired a boy who did not relinquish his enthusiasms easily, said, "They were special cases, Jim. The German boy was the Ambassador's son whom we took in exchange for one of our boys who planned to study abroad. The Negro had been entered for his junior year, but he had been seriously injured, most unjustly, in a racial attack, and spent much of the year in a hospital. Naturally, we couldn't add to the injustice done him by denying him the senior year."

Jim flushed with embarrassment. This man was very kind to explain the exceptions without growing angry. "I'm sorry. I didn't know the facts," the boy said.

"I wish you'd known this rule of ours a year ago, Jim. Mr. Ironwood is especially interested in having students from the Village."

Jim stood as if paralyzed. The interview was over, but the enormity of this denial of his lifelong ambition made it almost impossible for him to accept it at once. Dean Atwood, sensing this, said, "You mentioned baseball, Jim. Were you planning to make it your profession?"

Jim shook his head. "Not as a player, but a coach maybe. Our hired man played for the Phillies until he got injured, and he's filled me up with the game."

Dean Atwood, a specialist in boys, had been studying this one closely and he was impressed. "We honor all-out devotion here, Jim. I'd offer to take your special case up with Mr. Ironwood, but I know his answer right now. We have to say this disagreeable "No" at least once a week."

"I see—you can't," Jim made himself say, for he wanted to measure up to the Dean's spirit.

"I hope our refusal won't destroy your interest in Ironwood School," the Dean said, as his son yanked at his arm, impatient to keep moving.

"Nothing could do that."

"Please feel welcome to use any part of our plant that you may find helpful."

"Thank you," Jim replied, and turned away, for the kindness in the Dean's attitude was reducing his self-control. But he had gone only a few steps before he looked back and called out, "Do you know Laurie's last name, sir?"

"Yes, Anderson. She's a junior."

"Laurie Anderson," Jim repeated to himself. He'd have no trouble in remembering that—or her.

Bogie waggled all over to show his gladness at having his master back to relieve him of his sentinel duty. When Jim barely noticed, the retriever wondered in his dog's mind what he had done wrong. He had refrained from secretly following his master, much as he had been tempted to do so. He had guarded the car, and indeed he had scared off three curious boys who had approached to inspect this unique object on ill-assorted wheels. Yet just now Jim had accepted these services without a pat, nod, smile, or even a good word. To Bogie, Jim felt like a cross "*No,*" a stranger, and he made the dog feel lonesome and homeless. This feeling brought back dim, sad memories of the horrible time before Jim had found him, starved and freezing, on the highway. He felt Jim yank the car back and around, but his master didn't make the bushes go fast. Bogie was miserable.

Jim drove slowly because he had to think this setback out before he faced the family at supper. The McNail family was like those musketeers Jean was reading about—all for one, and one for all. With reservations, that is. Jim had learned in earliest boyhood not to advertise his plans ahead; he would then not be interfered with by well-meaning parents. He had kept his hopes of a year at Ironwood a secret. He had had to tell them that he had applied to State College, since his parents naturally were concerned about his future. If Ironwood had accepted him and State did, too, he had planned to postpone State for a year. Now he was thankful he had kept the Ironwood prospect under his hat, for he had inherited a double share of pride—from his father and his mother. Humiliation was bad enough just between him and himself; multiplying it was intolerable.

As Jim stopped at the mailbox near the family's salesstand, he noticed that Jean was handing over the last of the strawberries to a truck driver. She saw her brother and called, "I've got it!" She waved a letter. "It's from State."

His sister could be depended on to know all his affairs, Jim thought sourly, and walked over. She took the trucker's money, then handed the envelope to Jim, saying, "Please open it, Jim. I'm dying to know, even though I'm sure they'll say yes."

He slit the envelope and one glance informed him of the worst. He handed the sheet to her.

"Oh, Jim!" she wailed. "The monsters! How *could* they! How *stupid* can they be?"

"They have thousands more applicants than they can take," Jim told her as calmly as he could.

"You're just like that Spartan boy," Jean said with a wave of admiration.

"What Spartan boy?"

"You know, the one who let the fox eat him up without letting on."

"Oh, that one!" Jim's rigidity relaxed a little. "No, I'm not like him."

"You are! You don't rave and call names. Suppose it had been Scott who got this letter. He'd kick out the side of the house."

"And quite sensibly," Jim approved. "Then his temper's over."

"I like your way best, Jim," Jean said quietly.

A customer interrupted just then, and Jim went back to his car.

2

Woe vs. Will

JIM PARKED under the great white oak beside the house, a tree that even lightning couldn't keep from its purpose. He loved that tree and, as with things one loves, some of its qualities had seeped into him and supported him in trouble.

A glance at depressed Bogie reminded Jim of his faithful admirer and he roughed the retriever up a bit. Bogie's feelings righted and Jim began to get a hold on his. Two body blows in twenty minutes—well, they shouldn't shake him. It was early to start the milking, but all the better. Scott and Uncle Frank would be glad to find their chore lessened, and they couldn't read his face if it was hidden under a cow's flank.

Jim was glad that his father had not installed milking machines for their small herd. There was nothing like pulling milk from the patient animal to calm one's own spirits. Jim's father made fun of city people who took pills to make them happy. "They ought to keep a cow," Bruce McNail said. "Cows are the original tranquilizers."

"Keep her where?" Scott had asked. "You couldn't keep a fat mouse in their apartments without overcrowding."

Jim appreciated his brother—at a distance and best when out of hearing. Their views differed on nearly everything: on the weather, on girls, on work. This last difference was lucky for Jim, for Scott loved farming better than he loved himself. He loved it as Jean's cat loved her just-born kittens. In particular, he loved Burnsbrook Farm.

This suited Jim to the depths of his being, for it freed him from any responsibility to stay with the farm. Not that he disliked life on his father's three hundred acres. They had given him sound health and the strength of arm and body that a baseball catcher must have. The demanding chores of Burnsbrook's gardens, pastures, and woods had sharpened Jim's naturally quick eye and fastened on him the habit of sticking with a duty until it was accomplished or he was honorably relieved.

But for this upstanding, quietly good-looking young boy, managing cows, chickens, and vegetables was not enough. He wanted to be with people, especially those about his own age, and most especially boys with a yen for games and competition. Jim's father and mother had endowed him with a Scottish will, unmovable as a pasture rock. Opposition, if of ordinary size, had small chance of defeating his will.

His competitiveness, unlike Scott's, was not chiefly for personnal satisfaction or gain. It was hardly individual. He preferred the games in which team spirit predominated, and, because he had been coached by Uncle Frank as a catcher, almost from childhood, he favored baseball over football and soccer, let alone track. Team spirit was the adding of your own individual skill and power to the individual skill and power of the rest of the players for one grand result desired by all on the team. He had not even begun to get enough of this at his Ironwood Village School. The building of such power fascinated him. This, he was feeling more and more strongly, was something he could do with joy for the rest of his life—it could become his lifework. Even now, when bruised by the double blow delivered by Dean Atwood and State College, his determination was untouched. Sitting there on his three-legged stool, he did not even bother to be angry at these obstacles in his way.

Jim's racing thoughts over the milk pail were scarcely interrupted by the arrival of Scott and Uncle Frank. Milking in separate stalls was not conducive to talking, and Jim was spared any cross-examination about the Ironwood game. The supper table would be another matter. With the milking done, Jim washed up slowly so that the family would be busy with their food. But his father was only carving the roast pork when he sat down. His mother was ladling out new peas and carrots and Jean was carrying in a huge dish of steaming asparagus, napkin-covered. Jean was never separated from a book for long, if she could help it, and Jim noticed that she was pressing a book to her side under her upper arm, even as she bore the asparagus in.

"What now?" he asked, nodding at the book.

"*Ivanhoe*, if you must know," Jean said.

Scott looked up. "I've a rake, too." Nobody laughed because there was a general feeling that Scott's feeble puns should not be encouraged.

"Cornier than usual," Mr. McNail observed. "But then you're good at corn, Scott. Which reminds me: on Monday the south lot ought to be harrowed."

"You're harrowing me now," Scott replied. Nobody even smiled. Scott looked at Jim and said, "You're more subdued than is good for you. Did Ironwood bite the dust?"

"Cliffside took it, 5 to 3." Jim kept his voice steady, as if it didn't matter.

The sound of the telephone ringing stopped any cross-examination. Jean, who always was first at the receiver, returned to the table saying, "For you, Jim—she's got a nice voice."

"Let's see," Frank Lafferty said, "would this be Dolly, Hilda, Gertrude, Evelyn, Franny. . . ?"

Jim hated to talk before an audience and the telephone was extremely public when the family was gathered in the inner kitchen, the McNails' usual dining room.

"I hope you don't mind," the voice said, and he recognized it instantly as belonging to Laurie Anderson, the name he wouldn't forget—and now the voice he wouldn't forget, either. She told him that Master Paul Atwood had left Ironwood for the weekend and she couldn't possibly wait that long to hear whether he was coming to Ironwood next fall. Jim explained the situation and it helped in his disappointment to hear her exclaim, "Oh, I'm so sorry! We're going to need a good catcher next year, and anyone who knows baseball the way you do must be good."

A dozen things were racing around in his head. Should he ask to see her again before school let out? And where? He had his own canoe. In the meanwhile, she was saying, "I do hope I didn't interrupt your dinner or anything."

"I appreciate your calling a lot. The way Mr. Atwood explained it, I guess it's the sensible way to keep the school spirit. But if you've looked up to something the way I've looked up to Ironwood . . . and almost got to become part of it . . . and can't ever, now, it's hard to take. But your phoning makes it a bit easier. I wish I could talk to you more about Ironwood. I've never really known anybody on the inside. . . ."

"Will you excuse me, the first bell's just rung," she interrupted, and it was like spilling a pail of chilly water on him. Then she added, "I hope to help at the Day Camp here this summer. I'll know next week."

She hung up before he could even express his wish for

a date, but he went back to the table in a happier mood than he had thought possible earlier in the evening.

"Excuse us, but we couldn't help hearing," Scott began in his bantering tone. "Your voice carries like a whippoorwill's. Why didn't you tell us, dear, that you wanted to attend Ironwood School."

Scott's "dear" was such an excellent imitation of their mother that Jean burst into giggles.

Mrs. McNail had not raised three children, countless animals, and generations of the flowers she loved, without noticing the most minute degrees of change. She was a better weather forecaster than her husband and an expert family doctor, because she could divine symptoms at the very start. Now she had become sensitively aware that Jim was hiding some uncomfortable secret, so she said, "Why must you tease your brother, Scott? Especially about something that is no business of yours."

"I was just sympathizing with Jim, Mom," Scott answered with a straight face. "If he wants to go to Ironwood–"

Mr. McNail looked both puzzled and impatient. "You usually talk sense, Scott. What's got into you? Jim'll be through with schools when he gets his diploma from the Village High in a couple of weeks. Then he heads for State College. So why Ironwood? And who's going to fork over the twenty-five hundred dollars Ironwood asks? Money's still not growing on trees."

"It grows on Scott's," Jean put in. "A nice shiny quarter on the top of every Christmas tree he sells. He made six hundred dollars grown on trees, and in December, too!"

"This is Communism!" Uncle Frank shouted–but he was laughing. "Everybody butting into everybody else's business. What about Ironwood, Jim, or is that your secret?"

"It's no secret now," Jim said, and he found he was relieved to get the matter off his chest. "I thought my grades weren't quite good enough to get me into State, and I wanted to play ball for Ironwood. I've saved up eight hundred dollars, Pop, and Ironwood gives scholarships to students who can't afford the whole amount. But it's all off. Ironwood won't take one-year students, and I just got State's turn-down."

This unexpected reverse sobered even jester Scott. Finally, Mr. McNail's quick mind broke the uncomfortable silence with, "Nothing's final, Son. You can repeat the subjects you've done poorly in at Village High and State will accept you a year from now, I'm sure. It's your own head and not the school that counts. But whatever possessed you to think that Ironwood was the solution?" "Poor Daddy!" Jean broke in with mock consolation. "Do you *always* expect people to be reasonable?"

"Yes, I do, not being a woman. Is it such a failing?" In spite of his derogatory clichés, Mr. McNail smiled fondly at his favorite child.

"Didn't you *know* that ninety per cent of your life is guided by emotion?"

Mr. McNail replied in assumed humility, "I'm sorry to hear it. But I'll try to reform."

"You can't!" Jean told him positively. "Any more than you can change your nice face. You're still ninety per cent emotion and can't help it."

"What've you been reading now?" Scott asked his sister.

"My physiology book," Jean retorted with a little lift of her chin. "And it's true. I've been watching. Everything said at this table tonight is emotion. You like to tease Jim. That's emotion. Jim hides his heartful of emotions. . . ."

"Name three," Scott said with a wink at Jim.

"Well, he was eager to know who phoned him. That's emotion. He came back looking happy. That's emotion. He hid his disappointment at the news from State. More emotion. Want me to go on?" She ignored Scott's look of resignation and continued, "Father's full of mingled emotions about Jim: he's scared at the thought that he might have been asked to spend so much money at Ironwood—but, of course, that's all off now. Then he's irritated at State, and he's kind of proud of Jim, too, for planning anything so original. And Mother's sorry for everybody, as usual, which is several emotions. And Uncle Frank's hiding some emotion we're not allowed to see. And Jim's most emotional of all because he's the one really hurt. . . ."

"Don't begin over again!" Scott yowled.

At that tense moment, a sharp rapping on the screen door was followed by the appearance of a broad-shouldered, long-armed, outdoors-looking youth with a crew cut and a wide grin on a sunburned face featured by a pair of keen hazel eyes.

"Just in time!" hospitable Mrs. McNail said. "Jean, will you clear the table while I bring in the dessert? Tony, pull that chair up beside Jim."

"I did time it pretty well," Tony observed when the huge and beautiful strawberry shortcake appeared. "Trust a Wayland for that." Then he asked Jim, "What happened at Ironwood? Chuck said Cliffside won."

"Most of it happened before I got there," Jim began.

"Oh, dear! My fault!" Jean exclaimed. "Bring on the emotion."

"Forget it," Jim said to his sister. And to Tony, "Ted Everson stopped a batted ball with his pitching arm and Ironwood lost the game because the sub pitcher was no good."

"If you can't beat them, join them," Scott said, apropos of nothing—and wondered why everybody but Mrs. McNail burst into loud laughter.

Tony Wayland looked from one to another. "What's so funny about that?"

"Excuse us, Mother," Mr. McNail said.

Jean explained to Tony, "Scott was just quoting Mother. That's her cure-all. But it's no cure this time, when joining 'em is what Jim actually wanted to do."

"Well, you can't get me to laugh at anyone who makes strawberry shortcake like this," Tony said. "Yes, please," he added when Mrs. McNail signaled whether he would like a second helping. "If you won't put me in the pigpen for it."

"Two helps is just a beginning," Jean assured him.

Jim opened his mouth to say something, then fed himself more shortcake instead. His family, unwittingly, had given him an idea that nearly raised him from his chair. But it was an idea he must keep to himself, as his father eternally advised. He must work on it, anyway. Funny how many emotions you could have without labeling them. Jean was right. He had been a procession of emotions all afternoon—his impatience to get to the game, his soreness at Jean's lateness, his disappointment at Ironwood's defeat, his delight in finding that girl who knew her baseball so surprisingly, his overwhelming disappointment at Dean Atwood's decision, the added blow of State's refusal, his disproportionate pleasure at Laurie Anderson's thoughtful phone call, which raised such undue hopes, and now the new turn his inmost ambition had taken.

The others were rising, and Uncle Frank said to Tony and Jim, "If you two'll come down to the barn till that shortcake settles, we can have a bit of battery practice. I've got to mend my milking-stool."

3

Part of an Idea

Uncle Frank Lafferty was only an uncle by common consent. He was born with a baseball in his left hand, as he told it, which was a natural way of signifying that he was to be a southpaw. His father had owned a small tract of land next to the McNail farm. Frank would not settle down to raising hogs, as his father decreed, but ran away to play professional ball when he was in his teens. He worked his way up from the low minors to the better ball farms and had been taken on the Phillies' string as relief pitcher, at a salary so far ahead of what he could have expected from the hog business that it turned his head.

"I wasn't too modest," he said to Jim once when the boy was old enough to hear some of the facts of Frank's life. "I reckon I was about one hundred per cent ego, with a bonus. 'You call it; I'll throw it,' was what I'd tell catchers. When it rained, I played poker, which took care of my money. And when I was thirsty, I made love to the bottle, which took care of my future. The bottle made me spunky—silly-spunky. One night in Clearwater, Florida, just when

I'd got a raise and was told to pack up to go on the road for an exhibition game or two, I got so spunky that I contested the right of way with a truck, and the truck won. That's why I limp. That's why I'm not wearing a Phillies uniform today. I never caught up with my future, thanks to the bottle. You can drink or you can be somebody, but not both."

Frank had returned to Pennsylvania to find that his parents had sold the farm to Bruce McNail. They had retired to Ironwood Village, where they had been smothered to death in the smoke of their burning home. Mr. McNail had offered Frank a job. The ex-baseball player accepted promptly. He had begun tossing balls to Jim as soon as his hands were big enough to hold one. Then Tony Wayland, who had become Jim's best friend in their tadpole-catching days, tossed balls, too, and, little by little, Frank had turned him into a pitcher.

Then human nature took a hand as the embers of Frank's ambition glowed warm again. If he couldn't be great himself, he'd make Tony Wayland great, and, since a great pitcher needed a great catcher, he'd make Jim McNail great, too. While Frank was hardly a wise man, even yet, he was wise enough to conceal this outgrowth of his ego from the two boys. He knew that they would resent the punishing disciplining they were in for if they guessed the personal reason he had for making them work. He talked ball and quoted the picturesque personalities he had met or watched. The endless possibilities of the greatest game on earth—Frank's estimate—kept their natural pride reinforced with a healthy eagerness to excel.

Back of the Burnsbrook barn, where the cow pasture was reasonably level and smooth, Jim and Tony spent most of the clear evenings during the daylight-saving months *working*. They considered it fun, although actually it was more strenuous labor than the farm chores which occupied them from milking to milking. Presently Tony's younger brother Chuck and Jim's sister Jean were old enough to join in. Roy Mason, the young Negro boy whose father worked for the Waylands and who was a year older than Tony, was asked to stand on the flat rock called third base. Friends of the McNail boys heard of what was going on and drifted out to the Farm to look things over, a few to stay, although most of them resented the before-game drills. Goat Edwards, who had suddenly outgrown the name of Peanuts by sprouting three inches in a year, developed an eye for shortstop. In fact, Scott McNail was about the only holdout in the neighborhood. He preferred to spend his free hours fishing or berrying or seeking company in the Village where, happily—from his point of view—the girls outnumbered the boys two to one.

The Lafferty language was strong but restrained. Mr. McNail had cleaned it up in the course of the years. "I'm harness-broke like the horses," Frank said to the boys who had come to play and whose vocabulary was sometimes careless, to put it mildly. "Dog-bite you, Tony, *dip* that arm, *lift* that leg, *shoot* where you look." And to Jim, "Blast you for a mule, boy, *watch* that ball, *roll* your wrists faster, *balance* your weight." Or to Roy Mason, "*Take* it easy, you fish-worm. Take—it—*easy*."

Frank's instructions gained their force through repetition. He literally *drilled* them into the boys' brains, evening after evening, week after week, month after month, year after year, until habit wore unforgettable furrows in his pupils' brains. He praised in very small doses, but he never made fools of them, never made them feel small, never tried to change their natures. They built up a respect for themselves by the perfecting of their abilities, a respect scrubbed clean of conceit.

On this warm May evening baseball practice was slow in starting. All that shortcake had to settle, and while Frank was working on his milking-stool, Jim fired one barrel of his double-barreled idea. "I know now what we've been working for all these years," he said to Tony and Frank.

"I supposed it was for fun," Tony said and dropped down on the grass, while Jim and Frank sat on a much-carved wooden bench.

"I could've told you any time," Frank said. "Both of you boys've been heading for a forty-thousand-dollar job with the Phillies and a cut of the World Series money."

"Man, you do look ahead!" Tony grinned.

Jim said, "He's not looking in my direction. Besides, what I want I want now—and that's a team. I want sport this summer. This big valley's deader than it need be through July and August."

"Not on the truck farms, in the hayfields and the orchards," Frank put in.

"Evenings are long," Jim countered. "We've got the core of a team here, with Tony pitching, me catching, Roy at third."

"That's right. All we need is about eight or ten other guys." Tony was not being funny, however. The fire was catching. "Chuck'll buy it fast. He'll hold down first base."

"That's four," Jim said. "Sam Slant's good at second, if we can pry him from the Village dump. He says he's going to build a car to beat mine—but I got to the dump first."

They all laughed. Then Tony asked Frank, "You'd coach, wouldn't you?"

"Nobody yet has ever stopped me from giving advice," Frank answered. "But you can't grow a team the way you grow corn. Some of the teams we'd be playing, like Clairton or Pebble Creek, aren't exactly catch-as-catch-can nines."

"It's for fun," Jim told him. "You just said you wanted Tony and me to win the World Series for the Phillies. How's for getting started with a little competition this summer?"

"I was warning, not objecting," Frank said.

"Bert Winnow's a bet for right field," Tony suggested.

"He has a lofty opinion of himself, but he can throw," Frank agreed.

"I'll go see him tonight," Jim promised.

Frank looked with covert admiration at his product—as he thought of Jim. The boy had natural determination, persistence; but Frank had coached him in promptness. And now he wished he hadn't. Jim was becoming too prompt. Frank underrated the long thought-processes that went on in advance of the seemingly headlong actions. Jim had had a vague dream of a team for two years and it was Dean Atwood's killing of a longer dream that had kindled him into speedy action.

The arrival of Roy Mason and Sam Slant enabled Jim to try out his plan on them, with favorable results. Both these boys, who were in their late teens, cheered the idea and began suggesting possible recruits. Presently, Frank told them that time wasn't staying to listen to them, and Jim said to Tony, "I'll hit anything you throw." That was the action-producing challenge which never failed.

It was not until nine o'clock that evening that Jim connected with Bert Winnow at Ironwood Village's most frequented street corner. He separated Bert from the other young idlers and explained his mission.

Bert considered the proposal for a minute, then asked, "What's in it for me, if I can round up an outfield?"

"Fun." Jim was not surprised at the question.

"The heck with that! I can find fun enough in this village."

"What I want is the best center field in Delaware Valley, and a left field as good. I suppose that you'll want right field."

"You suppose right. Hank Lloyd'd play center, if you let him bring his girl to cheer for him."

"He can bring a carload for all I care," Jim said. He had forgotten about Lloyd, who was a clean, fast man at center.

"Then there's Sid Gresham. He's a better than fair left fielder. I suppose your Uncle Frank'll coach."

"Try and stop him," Jim said happily. "He'd coach the frogs in our pond if he knew the language. But will Sid lay off the beer? Frank won't have that. He's a reformed alcoholic, you know."

Winnow shook his head. "Sid can't stand water—so he says."

"Then pass him up. Pop won't have any truck with drinkers. What about Sid's brother Bill?"

"Bill's pure and got a good right arm. I'll see him tomorrow. Want me to ask Lloyd and Bill?"

Jim did. He thanked Winnow and wondered, as his car jugged homeward, whether his new right fielder knew his own preferences. He tended to be wishy-washy. Most people called it changing your mind, but Jim was afraid that it went deeper than that. Winnow had just refused to play ball without gaining something from it, and then, probably for fear of being left out of something, had agreed to play for fun. He wasn't wishy-washy on the field, though.

Mist was gathering in the hollows as Jim drove along. It was late for a farmer's son, with early milking coming up. But Jim felt tireless these days. Bogie greeted him but knew better than to bark at this hour. He put his muzzle in Jim's hand, to be tickled under the chin. With an extra pat on the head, Jim said, "A big day, boy. Let's go to bed."

The pair went upstairs noiselessly. As Jim undressed, he

marveled at how much could happen in a few hours—his cherished plan of playing for Ironwood smashed, a swell girl met, a new baseball team in the blueprint stage. The turn-down by State College didn't bother him much now; the other unspoken half of his idea superseded all previous plans.

He noticed a penciled note on his pillow. Jean had written, "I can tell you: her voice is lovely. P.S. Now you can tell me something. J."

Jim chuckled at that postscript. Jean thought of everybody—especially of his girls. Well, she'd approve of Laurie Anderson. He leaned over and patted Bogie, who was already curled up on a mat beside the bed. "Maybe it wasn't such a black day, after all, boy," he said quietly. But as he pulled the sheet over him, he told himself not to be stupid. That Ted Everson looked like a very smooth guy.

4

Windfall Week

"GET WITH IT," was Jim McNail's usual state of mind and not infrequent expression, whether applied to himself, Bogie, or the cows on their way to the outer pasture.

"Get with it" summed up determination and hope. One spark of hope was all the incentive he needed, and Laurie's phone call, although a very small spark indeed, warmed during the next two days, when he and Tony Wayland set about assembling a baseball nine after work hours.

The work at Burnsbrook Farm bore small relation to the old-time farm slavery that Jim's father could remember. There were strenuous days in spring, when everything had to be done at once, and again in the fall, during harvest. But Bruce McNail and his wife had long ago determined that their children should be as free as possible for their studies and games. Uncle Frank was a team in himself, and when Scott had convinced his father that he would sue him for damages if he didn't let him, Scott, toil on the McNail estate, Jim was comparatively a free young man.

Brother Scott occasionally sat in on the recruiting sessions, while Jim and Tony discussed possible players. When these organizers discarded a player, Scott amused himself by standing up for the discard. At bottom, he was his brother's faithful friend, but he often proved his faithfulness by questioning Jim's reasoning. "Don't be too fussy," was his comment when the boys decided against Sid Gresham because of his overcolorful language. "Don't you know, too, nice guys finish last?"

"What's too fussy about it?" Jim retorted. "He'll be working out here and Jean'll be hanging around. I don't want her listening to Sid's foul mouth."

"Nor your mother, either," Tony put in.

Scott shrugged. "Most managers choose their players for their game instead of their grammar."

"You know," Tony put in, "it's as Uncle Frank says. A guy's all of a piece. If his talk stinks, his play's likely to."

"All right, all right," Scott yielded. "But I still think that coaches gauge a player by his arm rather than his tongue. I'll be interested to see how the new way turns out."

Tony and Jim had to laugh at Scott, who, they knew, was only fooling. Scott was as eager for Jim to succeed in his way of being happy as he was himself in spraying and ditching and making that roadside stand the most attractive in the county. Jean's summer wages for tending it were more than pin money, or even bowling-pin money. She actually bought more books than she could read.

For a week, Jim's hopes were scantily fed by accomplishment. Final examinations and end-of-school doings, plus intensive strawberry picking, hindered a combing of the vicinity. But Jim throve on opposition, thanks to his ancestry and family example. In addition, Uncle Frank's weekly remark had become part of the boy's make-up: "Livin's like walkin' cross-country—up and down and then up again—if you go on, that is."

Jim had accepted as a certainty that good fortune had to follow bad, "if you go on, that is." Nothing had ever jolted him so violently as his turn-down by Ironwood School. Yet look at what had followed! Finding a ball-loving girl like Laurie, and now seeing himself a manager of a ball team. So "Get on with it," he told himself.

A few days later, the owner-editor of Ironwood Village's weekly paper, Isaac Morse, telephoned Jim. "I hear you're getting up a local ball team, Jim, and I'm for it," he said. "It's high time that Ironwood Village was back on the baseball map. Give me the facts, will you?"

"Will you be in your office for a while?" Jim asked with a pounding heart. This was the break he needed.

"For the morning. Come on in."

So Jim, Tony, and Bogie walked into the newspaper office thirty minutes later. Mr. Morse was on the telephone. Tony looked at the organized clutter of desk, newspaper files, shelves of reference volumes, and other paraphernalia of a country press, and said quietly to Jim, "The next time Mom tells me to redd up my room, I'll bring her to see this."

"What do you suppose that means?" Jim indicated a framed motto on the wall, "Desire is hidden identity."

Tony shook his head. "Unless it means you can savvy what you are by what you like."

"Then we're a couple of baseballs," Jim said. "It must mean more than that."

"I like that one," and Tony pointed out the advice, "You can't get experience by ducking it."

Jim laughed. Then he said, "There's one Pop would go for."

Tony read aloud, "A man never speaks of himself without loss." He looked puzzled. "I don't get it. You've got to talk out about yourself sometimes."

"When?" Jim asked. "Pop never does. He never says he's sick or well or happy or worried. He praises Laurie and Scott and me when we need a boost, but I've never heard him praise himself."

"Well, I guess it's true about most people," Tony admitted. "Take that blowhard, Curt Eames. Nobody even listens to him any more."

"He does overdo it a bit," Jim said, with his usual pleasure at understatement. "Pop calls him a 'drum'—so hollow he makes a noise easily."

Tony poked Jim in the ribs. "There's the best one of all!" He nodded at a long motto that recommended, "Half of your interest in people is that you can't figure them out, so don't give yourself away."

Jim only half agreed. "I don't like tightwads, though. Guys who won't come across with anything."

It was then that Isaac Morse hung up and greeted the boys.

Forty minutes later, with only six telephone interruptions, Jim and Tony walked out of the office greatly encouraged, and on the following Friday, Jim found himself in *The Village News* as "Captain Jim McNail" and the write-up ran as follows:

> Thanks to the initiative of James A. McNail of Burnsbrook Farm, aided by Frank Lafferty and Tony Wayland, Ironwood Village is to have a free-lance baseball team. This is all to the good. Softball is great fun, and this paper has been properly enthusiastic over Ironwood High's excellent showing in track, but the national game has no rival in the warm months. Even our splendid basketball teams of the past few years have not created the healthy interest that we once had

here in basketball. We know that our Valley springs are late and make the season for baseball short. But the High used to excel in the nine-inning game, now shortened to seven innings.

However, the inevitable change-back has come, and if Captain Jim has the success we think likely, baseball may again be the talk of the town—and this sheet. Watching the games at Ironwood School, during that short season, is no substitute for our own games. Old-timers dimly remember the day when the Village team played Ironwood School. May that time come again, because honorable rivalry makes for healthy relations.

The tentative line-up of the McNail team is as follows:

Tony Wayland,	pitcher
Jim McNail,	catcher
Bert Winnow,	1st base
Bill Gresham,	2nd base
Roy Mason,	3rd base
Henry (Goat) Edwards,	shortstop
	right field not yet chosen
Lew Lowbridge,	center field
Sam Slant,	left field
Belt Burrows,	sub catcher
Rink Davis,	sub pitcher

As expected, this announcement, prominently boxed on Page 1, brought a stream of telephone calls from hopeful volunteers. Mrs. McNail took down names, ages, supposed abilities, and the phone numbers of these inquirers, with whom Jim conducted interviews, also on the telephone. But an event stemming from an unlooked-for quarter shortchanged these potential right fielders.

Jim was working the roadside stand on a Saturday and, since the day was sunny, business had been brisk during the morning. Customers dropped off by midafternoon, however, and Jim had started checking receipts, when a car stopping made him look up. There sat Laurie Anderson beside the driver, and—more thrilling still—the driver was *not* Ted Everson, but a handsome young fellow with hair almost the shade of Laurie's.

She said, "I want my brother Dick to know you, Jim McNail. He plays ball, too."

As Jim shook the broad, hard hand, he noticed that Dick also had the masculine equivalent of Laurie's blue eyes. "This is better than okay," Jim said. "We're about sold out. We'll go up to the house for something to eat, if you can spare the time."

"That's easy," Dick answered promptly. "I was born hungry and have been ill-fed ever since."

"He looks starved, doesn't he?" Laurie asked.

But when Dick got out of the car at the McNail front door, Jim found no signs of emaciation. Laurie's brother was reaching for six feet and looked bronzed and fit. Jim asked him where he had picked up the sun-tan.

"Need you ask?" The boy grinned. "If I didn't play ball, Laurie would report me to the police."

"He's a fair hitter, a better runner, a really cool fielder, and not very happy on the bench," Laurie reported.

"Anything is right with me," Dick answered. Then he looked at his sister. "How're you going to square that with my boss?"

Laurie explained that her brother would be working at the Lake House, run by Ironwood School, during the summer. And she confirmed her hope that she was going to be working for the Day Camp. This news was the one item needed to complete Jim's happiness. Then Laurie would be at hand. Now if Ted Everson only had a job in Alaska . . .

But he didn't, Jim found out three seconds later. "The

Lake hours are divided into three shifts," Laurie was telling Dick. "Ted will see that you manage the afternoon shift off." Her tone indicated that she could manage Ted. Jim's heart ran a beat slower. But Dick looked like a find—he was probably seventeen, certainly easygoing, and perhaps he might not have what it takes to hold down the right-field position. But he was certainly going to have the chance to show his ability—or lack of it.

To Jim's surprise, the kitchen's screen door had been propped open. "Gosh, the place will be full of flies!" he exclaimed. "My sister's been reading a book. She forgets everything else." But he had barely stepped inside when he backed quietly out. "*Sshh!* We have a guest."

The two Andersons peeked in and saw a skunk curled up in front of the stove. "Lucky I noticed him," Jim said, "or we all might have had to bury ourselves in the woods."

They retreated to the shade of a broad-branched maple. "How far can he throw it?" Dick asked.

"Across our kitchen anyway, and after that nobody could live in there for days, maybe weeks. Nature went all out to protect that animal." Jim whistled Bogie to him, threw his bandanna on the grass and said, "Watch it." Then, in an undertone to the others, he explained, "That'll anchor him."

"Does this happen often?" Laurie asked with a giggle.

"This is a first for us," Jim stated. "Skunks mind their own business better than most people. Tony Wayland, who pitches for the new team, told me that a family of skunks lived under their back porch all one summer and made no trouble. The thing is not to startle them."

"You'd better come to the Village with us for those eats," Dick suggested.

"I must get the creature out before someone barges into him," Jim said.

"But how?" Laurie asked. "If we sounded the horn, would he come out?"

"He'd waken, anyway. That's a good idea." Jim got to his feet ahead of Dick and blew a blast. Then he went to the kitchen window and waited. When he returned to the Andersons, he reported, "I reckon he considered that horn none of his business. He's still curled up. Our day is his night, of course. If you don't mind waiting a few minutes, I'll see if I can smoke him out."

"May we look?" Laurie asked.

Jim nodded. "Stand by the far window."

The Andersons took up their position and Jim brought a fire bucket from the shed, emptied out the water on the grass, stuffed some old newspapers, also from the shed, into the bucket, broke up a few twigs from the dry underside of a spruce tree, lit the paper, and when the wood caught fire, tossed some of the dampened grass onto the blaze. Thick smoke boiled up. Dick took the screen from his observation window and lowered the bucket to the floor. Then he quickly rejoined the watchers at their window, taking Bogie with him.

At first the sleeping animal seemed undisturbed, but as the smoke billowed to the ceiling and worked downward, the skunk twitched, raised his head, stared around, sniffed, rose, and stood still. Dick said quietly, "That's right: walk, don't run, to the nearest exit." This the skunk did, ambling slowly toward the opening to a purer atmosphere outside.

By now Bogie was making noises in his throat as his master held his collar firmly. Jim asked Dick to take the screen out of their window, thus making a cross draught. "It's lucky Bogie wasn't off exploring and galloped back unexpectedly. His I.Q. is no match for his inherited instincts, and Burnsbrook Farm would be smelling to heaven by now."

"Don't even farm dogs learn sense?" Dick asked.

Jim shook his head. "Not about skunks or porcupines. A dog is the most overrated creature that we can't do without. I don't know where that leaves us."

"Well, we're not so spectacularly rational either," Laurie said.

"My sister was telling us the other evening that we are ninety per cent emotion and the rest intellect." Jim smiled. "And she proved it by what we'd been saying."

"My dad says the same thing," Dick put in. "He says that if you'll remember that we're not very reasonable, you'll be helped with getting on with people. Actually he said with women."

"As if women *could* be more unreasonable than men!" Laurie exclaimed.

"Well, you've just seen one man reason his kitchen out of some hard luck!" Dick countered.

"Yes, and I think you're wonderful!" Laurie said with unabashed candor to Jim. "I wish Mr. Ironwood could have seen you handle this. He's mad about brains."

"I wish mine made more impression on schools," Jim said with equal candor. "Let's change the subject. If you'll sit down in the shade here, I'll open up the house to let out the smoke and bring out the eats as advertised. What do you like? Mom keeps a food bank for emergencies like this," and he named some of the staples.

"Go no further," Dick said. "Apple pie and root beer, and I'll come help. I've got a porter's license."

Laurie settled for the same, and Jim brought out a soup bone to keep Bogie busy. It was cool in the shade of the great maple, and presently Dick said, "Boy, this is the life! How long does it take to become a farmer?"

"About three generations." Jim grinned past a forkful of pie.

Laurie looked at her wrist watch. "We have a date," she said to her brother.

"You mean you have. Ted would give me anything but that convertible if I didn't drag along."

Jim felt a cloud settling on his happiness: he had forgotten Ted Everson. Laurie said to Jim, "Ted told me that he'd seen a piece in the paper about you and a ball team you're getting up. Is that true?"

Jim nodded. "Tony Wayland and I have been pitching and catching since we were kids, with just pick-up games when we could get a crowd. Now we want to cash in on all that practice with some fun. Thanks to *The Village News* publicity, we've rounded up a team, or most of one. We still need a right fielder." He looked at Dick. "If you'd like that spot, you're on. Or you could sub for almost any position. Somebody's sure to drop out. What have you played?"

"Most anywhere," Dick said a little too casually to please Jim. "Right field would be fine."

"Look," Jim broke in, "the team's coming out here for first practice this evening. Why don't you stay to supper and try out with us?"

"The winning point!" Dick exclaimed. "Ted gets Laurie. I get off being third cartridge in a double-barreled gun. You get a right fielder—I hope. And Laurie gets her wish."

"You don't know what I wish," Laurie said while a flush warmed her cheeks. She rose. "Jim, you're the most generous person! I can't thank you enough for giving Dick a try, and the root beer's delicious. When should I come for him?"

Jim wanted to say, "When it gets too dark to play," but she had just called him "the most generous person" and shortening her evening with Ted was scarcely generous. It was small, and being small wasn't his way; besides, it never paid. So he told her, "Most of the boys come from the Village and Dick can get a ride in."

Laurie slipped into her car and Jim closed the door. "You must come see us practice," he said. "My sister Jean will be company for you, and Tony's sister, too."

"I'd like nothing better. The Day Camp's day is over at four, and I'd love watching you practice."

When Ted Everson permits, Jim thought, but he did not say it aloud.

5

How to Build a Ball Team

JIM WAS ENCOURAGED, not to say secretly relieved, to have his team and subs appear at the McNails' farm on time and without hangers-on, as requested. He and Tony knew most of them well, and the others at least well enough to speak to on meeting. Dick Anderson was the sole stranger, and his open nature, plus a desire to make good, proved a satisfactory recommendation to this mixture of farmers' sons and small-town frequenters. Dick Anderson's accustomed civility might have been a superficial drawback to the others, whose manners were of the rough, direct variety, if it had not been associated with an obviously able body.

Jim had asked each recruit to bring whatever baseball equipment he owned, and most of the team arrived with bats, mitts, balls, and working clothes. He led them to the pasture lot behind the barn and said, "If there is anyone who doesn't know it, Uncle Frank Lafferty is dictator here. He's spent the last ten years teaching Tony Wayland and me all we know—with a bat." He felt his scalp tenderly and the rest laughed. "I turn you over to him now."

Frank regarded his material with an experienced eye. His voice was hard-grained, his dark eyes had a penetrating power, and his mouth promised firmness, but the ends turned up, as if accustomed to smiles. He said, "If I really was a dictator here, Jim and Tony would be working at a Phillies' farm, instead of heaving rocks and pulling cows' teats."

This of course brought a laugh. Frank went on, "I've got three things to drive home in this inning: First, we're out for fun. Second, fun, and I mean satisfaction, depends on how honestly you work as an individual. Third, teamwork is more satisfying than anything one individual can achieve alone. Now as a start, I'll knock out balls to you in your various positions, and you fire them back to catcher Jim as straight and fast as you can. Let's go."

The next forty minutes spoiled some local reputations and made others. Boaster Bert Winnow, at first base, kept Jim jumping for the returned balls, couldn't keep them down. Uncle Frank, backing up Jim, had a foghorn's vocal delivery. He shouted to Bert, "Overhanded, man! Grip the ball across the seams, and throw it with a full arc, overhand." Then Frank said to Jim, "We've got to bat ground balls to him until he can charge the ball better. He's got to come up with it, roll it to grip the seams, and throw it overhand in a split second."

"Maybe all that'll choke off his gab," Jim muttered. "He's the biggest blowhard in the bunch."

"Just so he uses his arms and legs right, I don't care about his mouth," Frank said. "At least it proves he isn't asleep."

Dick Anderson, tryout for right field, had the aristocrat's ease of manner. He looked comfortable. "He's a left-hander and that's good," Frank said to Jim. "It's a seconds-saver not to have to turn to throw in. The question with these easy guys is have they the will to win." Frank stopped a wide throw from second and said, "It's the happy boys who need the harness."

"I'll harnes him," thought Jim, but said nothing. He was more interested in Dick's making good than he would have admitted, even to Frank, to whom he could say anything and be understood. When Jim looked at Dick, what he saw in his mind's eye was Laurie. Jim was relieved to find Dick could give a ball lots of carry, although he was hardly a sharpshooter. He needed to loosen up a little. His tightness probably came from the nervousness of strangeness, when everyone else knew all the others.

"Lucky that the spot open was right field," Frank said. "He'll have to wake up on the getaway. He seems loose enough before the ball reaches him, but doesn't tighten up his attack. That's a long throw to third, but I think he's good for the distance. Anyway, he's no nail-chewer, you can see that."

Bill Gresham, slated for second base, pleased Jim and Frank. "He just naturally covers ground," Frank pointed out. "Watch him take this grounder," and Frank knocked a sizzler along the turf. Then he called to Gresham. "That's right, Bill. Grab your ball sure before you throw it, then get it away fast. A bobbled ball mostly loses a play. Which way do you move easiest? To your right or left?"

"Neither," Bill shouted back and the others laughed.

"Try this," and Frank knocked a fast one so that Bill had to jump to get it. The ball tipped his glove and rolled on, but Bill recovered cleanly and burned it in.

"Now this," and Frank sent an equally hot one to Bill's left. The boy stopped it neatly and returned it straight.

"There's your answer," Frank called. "Practice fast balls to your right."

Lew Lowbridge, center field, was long-armed and long-legged but hardly long-headed. "There's your problem child," Frank said to Jim. "More concentration needed." Then he called to Lew, "Get going faster, man! Get under the ball. Watch it as it leaves the bat and get the jump on it."

"How do you do that? I'm watching."

"You're above it!" Frank explained. "Crouch so that you see on a level with my swing. In a game, you've got to watch the batter for the groove. Your legs are the spring of the trap and your hands its jaws. More balls are going to fall in for hits than you can catch up with unless you break fast. You've a big territory to cover. And don't forget to call for flies."

Then to Jim, "We've got to give part of every practice to getting them used to calling for flies. It's almost as important as the other phases of fielding—and gets ignored. Yet I've seen it save games, win them."

After a few more balls to Lew, Frank said, "We may have to bench him unles he wakes up. He's a star-gazer."

"What do you mean?"

"Lets his mind wander—to his girl probably. I kind of wish they'd hurry up with that ferry to the moon and take the girls with them during the ball season."

"Woman-hater!" Jim gibed. "What's the matter with having a girl come and cheer for you? That wins games."

"If you ask me what wins games between teams evenly matched, I'll tell you—and it's not girls. It's concentration. Keeping a target eye on every play. Indifference is premature death, on or off the field. You can't divide eagerness between ballplaying and some skirt on the side lines. Do you suppose a wounded moose standing off a pack of wolves is thinking of some she-moose in the bushes? No sirree, one thing at a time."

"Just the same, if my girl was on the moon, I'd worry about her." Jim liked to egg Frank on.

"You and your girls!" Frank retorted.

Roy Mason was Frank's cure for all moods, whether of impatience, despair, or whatever. He was big, supple as only a Negro can be, and utterly without fear. It was difficult to believe that he was not yet eighteen. He looked a man, acted the man, and his memory was letter-perfect. Roy had played with Jim and Tony through the seven years that his father had been working for Mr. Wayland. He had been as grateful for Frank's free coaching as Frank was for the gifted pupil. Frank had told Tony once, "If I wanted to act mean to your father, I'd tell Roy to drop hoe and harrow and hunt up a job in the minors. He's pretty nearly as good as a lot of third basemen I've seen drawing down big pay."

"He'd tell you he'd think about it," Tony had replied. "Lots of people have tried to bribe him away from the farm, but he won't budge. He's free, independent, and one of us; it keeps him smooth and happy."

"Maybe I could use him to coach the others in glove-work," Jim suggested.

"Do that," Frank said. "If you can get them to lower their gloves, the way Roy Mason does, you've saved many a run. Roy never waits for the bounce."

Shortstop Goat Edwards, the short-short shortstop, according to Scott, who had stopped to watch, had grown a thick skin because of being perpetually reminded of his lack of height. Just the same, he was a keen player and had mastered a quick delivery of the ball. He had mastered the art of gripping the ball across the seams and cocking his wrists to give it a snap as it left his hand. Also, he gave the ball that little extra velocity so useful in a pinch-throw. Goat had applied his sense of humor, originally thrust on him, to the double play, which was a sort of practical joke itself. He had developed a sidearm throw, too.

"What he needs now is to work on pop flies," Frank told Jim. "He could pep up his relay work, too."

"Oughtn't he to play closer to third base?" Jim asked. "That way, he'll hold runners on the bag longer."

"I agree," Frank said. "We've got a laster in him."

Goat interested Jim by the way he shed the kidding. It seemed to add to his popularity. Jim, like any normal youth, hoped for a sound popularity, though Frank said it was poison. To Jim, it seemed like savings in a bank. You didn't think about it, but it was there for use in an emergency.

Frank gave Sam Slant out in left field his share of flies and found that Sam knew what was expected of him. He covered his ground adequately and got the ball back to Jim fast and cleanly.

With dusk only half an hour away, Frank called for a game. Half a dozen extras had accumulated on the side lines to watch, and Frank enlisted them as batters and runners. Tony tried his own little game with himself—to pitch two enticing but deceptive strikes, and then an easy ball that any fair batter could hit. The new nine played well enough to feel encouraged, and when darkness called the game, Mrs. McNail invited them to enjoy a snack of pie à la mode and root beer, which Jean, Scott, Frank and Jim served to the players seated on the grass just outside the kitchen door.

Frank took the occasion to say, "This has been a business-like evening. Now, as Mrs. McNail will tell you, a kettle needs a lid for a quick boil. Which means that we need opposition to develop fast. Jim is going to write around, asking for games. We ought to meet here three nights a week until July. If each of you will bring in one extra player who doesn't mind waiting for you to get hurt, it will be good insurance. A man waiting to step into your shoes keeps you on your toes."

"Has the team a name?" Dick Anderson asked.

"We've been calling it *Jim's Team,*" Tony Wayland said.

"And Jim gives that idea a short ride to the dump," Jim said.

"Let's call us *The Winners,*" Bert Winnow suggested. "That's what we aim to be."

"And get the pants kidded off us if we lose!" Sam Slant exclaimed. "No, sir."

"Why not *The Burnsbrookers?*" Dick Anderson suggested.

There was a silence. Anderson was a stranger, but he had won their respect during the evening by his fielding and an entire lack of conceit.

"That's pretty long, isn't it?" Jim questioned.

"I'm for it," Bill Gresham said decidedly. "All in favor say *Aye.*"

"*Aye*" shouted the crowd loudly enough to startle the dozing birds. Then, after thanking Mrs. McNail for the refreshments, the boys started for their cars.

Jim found a seat for Dick Anderson in Bill Gresham's bus. "I hope you can fix up the time with your boss," he said. "And if you can bring Laurie, all the better. She'd have Jean for company, and she's got to come to the games."

"You couldn't keep her away—and thanks for cutting me in on this, Jim. It's going to make my summer."

That night, in bed, Jim reflected how situations could change beyond prediction. He had a team—or at least the makings of one. He had Laurie's brother as a beginning friend. He had Laurie in the neighborhood and the coming games as lure, nor could Ted Everson do much about that. And he had started to bring about the other half of his big idea. . . . Then sleep took over.

6

How to Kill a Ball Team

THE FOURTH OF JULY opened hot, according to custom in the Delaware Valley. During the morning, the humidity thickened. The midday meal, at eleven-thirty, was a quiet affair for the MacNail family. The weight of the Burnsbrookers' first game lay heavy on Captain Jim's shoulders. The team wanted a victory, deserved a victory, needed a victory as a reward for the faithful practice during June. And to Jim personally a victory was essential in order to lead up to the triumph he was dreaming of, but had mentioned to nobody. Perhaps a year from now—

Even Scott had the grace to stuff himself with calves' liver, bacon, new peas, buttermilk, and fresh cherry pie without too many sarcastic broadsides, although he did say, as he passed his plate back for a second piece of pie, "You remember, Jim, where nice guys finish."

"How do you know?" Jean asked her brother with some irritation because it was hot and she admired Jim so much and, above all, wanted him to come through the afternoon with a smashing big score. "How *do* you know? You've never been one since Jim got up his team."

"That's a rather broad statement," Scott said with a grin. It tickled him to needle Jean because she could hold her own.

"Stow it," Jim told his sister. "We'll show him."

"I don't know what you're talking about," Mrs. McNail said.

"Scott's favorite joke is that nice guys finish last," Jim informed his mother. "He doesn't mean it."

"Well, I should hope not!" Mrs. McNail exclaimed.

"Scott's dead right!" Mr. McNail amazed everybody by stating. "That is, if by being nice he means decent, generous, just, and obedient to his principles. He's the very guy who does finish last—I mean he *lasts*. What's more, he builds up a power in him that others feel and come to rely on. Like Scott himself. We've never relied on him in vain."

"Pour some iced tea on my blushing map!" Scott said and draped a napkin over his head. Jean clapped her hands in glee.

"You said it!" Uncle Frank said to Mr. McNail. "The nice guy respects the other guy's personality, gets to know him, and knowledge is always power, always. The nice guy never takes advantage and so he doesn't build up animosity against him. The nice guy doesn't blow his top in a jam because that kind doesn't scare. You ought to know, Scotty, being one of them."

"You don't often hit below the belt, Frank," Scott said.

A sound of cars arriving ended the duel. Dick Anderson had Laurie beside him and three of the team in the back. The Wayland car brought Roy Mason and Garry Steep, a friend who was interested in the team. Bert Winnow's jalopy carried others. Frank Lafferty's car was to take the bats and other equipment and Jean offered to ride with him. Mr. McNail couldn't go, so he offered to keep Bogie with him.

"What, my mascot, Pop?" Jim was horrified. "Bogie's got baseball manners. He never bites more than one leg off a bad umpire." Jim opened the door and Bogie jumped into his car, where Laurie sat, by invitation, with Scott, Goat Edwards, and Bill Gresham.

Bill handed a copy of *The Village News* to Jim, saying, "Ike Morse has given us a swell send-off. Have you seen it?"

Jim hadn't and asked Laurie to read it while he drove. Laurie read aloud:

> "*The Burnsbrookers* play Clairton tomorrow, July 4, on Clairton Fairgrounds, at 2 P.M. We have witnessed some of the team's practices at the team's birthplace, Burnsbrook Farm, and Coach Frank Lafferty has done wonders at licking the nine into shape. Clairton is very proud of this year's team, undefeated so far, and is calling for a massacre. Jim aims to oblige. "Judge" Oarsley will umpire. The batting order has not been definitely settled, but the following players will start:
>
> "Jim McNail, captain and catcher
> Tony Wayland, pitcher
> Bert Winnow, 1st base
> Bill Gresham, 2nd base
> Roy Mason, 3rd base
> Henry (Goat) Edwards, shortstop
> Dick Anderson, right field
> Sam Slant, left field
> Lew Lowbridge, center field
> Subs: Joe Chapman, Belt Burrows, Rink Davis."

Jim properly concealed his elation at having *his* team acknowledged publicly in this way. Newsprint had transferred his imagined club to reality. Now they must make good. Last night, when Frank had talked over the prospects with Tony Wayland and him, he had said, "You two make the hard core of example to the others. It takes only one queen bee to hold a hive together, and the team has you both to follow. I'm not scared of you losing your heads."

To make Jim's joy deep, if not complete, Laurie was not only a most attractive girl openly being nice to him, she was a keen-eyed sharer of his fortunes. She knew good ball from bad, and he intended to show her how well his team could work under pressure—if only the storm would hold off. His farmer's eye had spotted the growing cumuli on the horizon, but this was a common occurrence in that foothills country, and often no storm developed.

The Clairton Fairgrounds simmered in shadeless heat, but two or three hundred spectators had collected, using their cars as "grandstand" seats. Jim's team threw the ball around and then gathered about Frank while Clairton tossed a few.

"Get a load of that pitcher," Bert Winnow said.

"Bet his Pop was a giraffe," Rink Davis asserted.

Tony, who had been watching the delivery, said, "That fellow's dangerous. He gets his whole length into it."

"Let's hope it's all looks," said Bill Gresham.

"Like those shirts," Dick Anderson declared. The admired shirts were scarlet with yellow letters proclaiming CLAIRTON diagonally across the front.

"We ought to have something like that," Rink Davis said.

"That screams!" Jim declared. "Wait till you see what the girls have doped out!"

Frank Lafferty had taken a paper from his shirt pocket and now he announced, "Here's the batting order that Jim and I have worked out. Not necessarily final. We're anxious to have suggestions for improvement. Roy Mason leads off because he's shown himself best at getting on base. Bert Winnow's next, as he's a right-field hitter and so can hit behind Mason on his way to second. Third comes Jim, for he's the next best hitter after Sam Slant, who'll be number four—to bring the three men on base home."

"Good idea!" Tony said and got a short laugh.

"Goat Edwards follows Sam. He's the steadiest of you all, so far. Lew Lowbridge next. He sometimes sees it and sometimes not, but he's got to see it today. Seventh, Dick Anderson, our best base runner. Eighth, Bill Gresham, who hits well behind the runner. Finally, Tony Wayland, who's got orders to run no bases in a hurry."

They snickered at that and did not need Frank's explanation—that pitchers must save themselves for pitching. "It ought to take all they've got. Watch the pitcher on your next TV game, and you'll see what I mean. A man can't do himself in sliding for the bag and come to the mound fresh and loose. Now what's my last word?"

"Glue your eye to the ball!" several voices chanted while the rest laughed. They had heard it before—a few hundred times.

The Clairton pitcher had taken his warmup and Roy Mason stepped into the box. Jim hoped that Roy could get those boxer's shoulders of his into a hit. Clairton would never find the ball. Roy limbered up with a couple of swings, held his bat back and waited. The pitcher let fly with a sinker—of all first pitches! It neared the plate like an ordinary fast ball and then took a reckless dive. Roy swung—but inches above. The crowd shouted approval. "Do it again, Beans!"

"String-bean," Goat commented.

"Whiplash," Jim said. "It's a wonder his arm doesn't sound."

The pitcher shot his second in; Roy ducked.

"Good watching!" Frank said. "That ball would have removed his head if it had connected."

"I don't like this guy," Dick Anderson commented.

"Don't cry before you're hit," Bert Winnow said.

"Nobody's crying," Jim said.

The pitcher cranked up again, placed the ball on target but forgot to put his stuff on it. Roy sliced a drive between shortstop and third base. The left fielder met it and slammed it across to first in a mighty throw, but Roy had turned the corner and was stampeding toward second when the first baseman jumped for a catch, came down set to throw and threw to second.

"*Slide . . . Slide!*" shouted Frank, and Roy slid—safe by a hair, as the Burnsbrook bench saw it.

The umpire signed him for out. Instantly, Jim's team and the others with them roared out their indignation. Winnow dashed out onto the field, with Lowbridge and Gresham following. But Frank, Jim, and several others shouted these hotheads back.

"What's the matter with you guys?" Winnow called angrily. "That ump's a lunkhead thief. You going to take it lying down?"

"Button it up, Bert," Tony warned. "Do you want to break up the game before it's started?"

Roy joined them. "I was safe—I know it," he said.

"Sure, we saw that much," Dick Anderson told him.

Jim said to Winnow, "You're up. Now's your chance to get back at them the right way."

"Cool off," Frank told him. "Coolness does it."

"And it can't be much over a hundred in the shade," Goat added.

They watched Bert carry his bat at the ready to bean the umpire, and because he was fuming inside, the pitcher had no trouble with him at all. A fast one, low and inside—a still faster one, even lower and still inside. Two strikes in no time at all. Bert turned and glared at the umpire but fortunately did not speak. The pitcher nailed him with the third throw—that illusive sinker. Bert heaved his bat halfway to the bench and called the umpire an offensive name. That official walked to the visitors' bench and said to Frank, "He's through. I don't have to take that mouth and won't. I could order him off the field, but won't. I'm as sorry for this as you are. Now let's have a ball game."

"And he doesn't mean b-a-w-l," spelled the Goat when the umpire was out of hearing.

"All right, fellows," Jim said. "We're off to a bad start; let's forget it and show them we came here to play ball."

"We mustn't let Ike Morse down," Tony Wayland said. "His car's just come. You're up, Jim. Let's save this inning."

Jim swung two bats, dropped one, walked to the plate, and tried to quiet the echoes of Bert's raucous voice in his mind. The pitcher, starting from his toes and moving up his long legs and limber body to that whiplash arm, produced a cannonball. Jim's eye never left it until his bat met it fairly. The crack told all. The ball flew almost parallel to the ground just over the shortstop, then rose, whistled at the left fielder below and vanished over the Fairgrounds fence.

Jim loped around the circuit and evaded as many of the hands pounding his back as possible. Laurie and Jean called to him excitedly. He grinned and called back, "That's what we came for, wasn't it? Watch Sam do number two!"

Sam Slant had reached the box and Jim knew that he was nervous, because he stepped too close to the plate, then back, then tried an in-between stance, and the pitcher called, "Make up your mind, if you have any."

That was the pitcher's error. Sam's nervousness burned off and he met the pitcher's curve just right by stepping into it and connecting in one vigorous motion. The grounder evaded the pitcher's grab by a foot, and Sam was safe at first.

This was fine, this was dandy, Jim thought. They were

saving the inning. The Goat, looking rather stumpy and slender, hid any nervousness over his assignment by a rather jaunty stance at the plate. When the pitcher wound up, Sam Slant took an inviting lead. The pitcher did not accept the invitation but hurled a fast one down the middle. Goat smothered it to place a nice bunt at the right distance from everyone, and Sam reached second. When the shortstop threw, he had not gripped the ball firmly enough and the throw fizzled out before it reached first. Goat grinned, safe.

Lew Lowbridge missed twice then nipped the ball for a disastrous foul, which the catcher caught—and the side was out.

"All right, fellows," Jim said. "Let's make it fast. That sky doesn't look good to me."

It was obvious that a thunderstorm was organizing on the northwest horizon. It should, by all the signs, move toward the river and miss Clairton, but all that power sometimes didn't follow the rules. "There ought to be a weather umpire," Jim said to himself. He wanted above all things to beat Clairton fairly—for Frank's sake, for all their sakes, including the girls and Ike Morse.

Tony took his pitches to Jim and the first Clairton batter, a chap with a football physique, stood in the box. Jim signaled for an insider, low and fast, and Tony delivered per order. It worked, and then it worked again. Then Tony threw a neat sinker and the man was out.

For the next man up, Tony changed speed and the batter caught a small piece of it for what Frank called a fountain foul. Jim waited underneath and held it. The third Clairton man up hit Tony's first pitch for a liner, straight into Tony's mitt, and the side was down. Eight innings to go.

"Ten minutes," Frank said. "Do it in eight next time and we'll beat that storm."

The next three innings were comparatively uneventful.

The Clairton pitcher never threw a ball above the batter's stomach, and the Burnsbrookers got used to his speed—but at a cost of no runs. The Clairton fielding was sharp, and while Dick Anderson and Jim reached third base in the fourth inning, they died there. Nor did Clairton score.

Meanwhile, the whole western sky slowly darkened. The hot south wind died. The gradually approaching tempest added a new tension to the growing strain of the game. The Clairton crowd became noisier in its disappointment at being behind. They were not going to take a beating quietly.

The fifth inning found Roy Mason up. The pitcher remembered how Roy had reached for his sinker and missed, so he tried it again. Roy passed: one strike. The pitcher repeated. Again Roy passed: strike two. The pitcher brushed off his catcher's signal, which Jim decoded as a command to throw a curve, and fired a third sinker. Roy connected with a mighty swipe, the ball started out and up. Roy reached first and the center fielder was still racing for the rolling ball. Roy tore down to second. Jim and Frank both shouted Slide, *slide*. Roy slid, overshot the bag, but reached back and tagged it before the second baseman tagged his arm. The umpire signaled an out.

Instantly, Bert Winnow, Lew Lowbridge, and Gresham were on their feet, protesting, and started out onto the field.

"Stop this!" Jim shouted and followed to try to dissuade these hotheads from starting a fight. The umpire, seeing them coming, waved them off the field. He might just as well have waved the approaching squall line of the thunderstorm to reverse itself. Clairton rooters began to pour out of their cars and rush onto the field. Someone threw a pop bottle from the side lines and hit Mason on the shoulder.

Frank, Jim, Anderson and the other Burnsbrookers were now doing their best to pull their angry teammates away from the umpire. The Clairton ball team rushed into the hassle. The melee became general, with the innocent being slugged along with the taunters. Jim, Frank, and Dick stuck together and helped Winnow and Lowbridge free themselves from the drubbing they deserved. The other Burnsbrookers, fighting a rear-guard action, fought off the jeering pack, helped by the cooler heads of the Clairton crowd. The town's handful of police finally completed the separation, but a roll of thunder, almost overhead, did more than the police to end the turmoil.

Frank and Jim hurried to the girls, but nobody had bothered them. "Oh, Jim, Jim!" cried Jean and burst into tears.

Laurie Anderson controlled herself but knew the blow that this sudden, unforeseeable fiasco was to Jim's hope. "It wasn't your fault!" she exclaimed shakily. "It wasn't, and you mustn't blame yourself."

Ike Morse joined them and said, "Too bad, Jim. I'll make it clear in my write-up who is to be charged with this most disappointing mess. I hope you'll rid the team of Winnow at least."

The tumult of storm wind, rushing from under a lurid arc of cloud, was announced by a bolt of lightning which must have struck nearby, with instant thunder. The gust broke over them, hurling large drops into their faces—and then the deluge descended!

"That'll cool them off," Roy said, pointing to the crowd rushing toward their cars, holding jackets over their heads.

"I hope it drowns them," Goat said. His nose was bloody and his right eye was swelling. The others on the team, clustering around, showed minor hurts and torn clothes. Even Garry Steep had suffered a cut on the cheek.

"The innocent bystander always gets killed first," Garry said. "I'm glad to be that much of your team, Jim."

Jim was silent, tense, busy getting his fellows to climb into the cars. The rain sluiced down, and, for a few moments, hail beat on the windshields and tops. Jim hoped that the belt of hail would not reach their fields. The roads were covered with water in places.

Laurie, sitting next to Jim, had the good sense to say nothing. She had seen enough of him by now to realize how much he had counted on this game, and to have the first victory for the Burnsbrookers snatched from him hurt him far more than the physical blows he had sustained. When she glanced at him, it hurt to see his set features.

He was thankful that he had to focus his attention on the driving and could postpone thinking about the disaster. He wanted never to see Winnow, Lowbridge, or Gresham again! The others he could forgive; they had been sucked into the melee. Tony and Roy had kept their heads and protected Bert and Lew from serious injury. Frank had explained the situation to the police satisfactorily. But that didn't help. *The Clairton Weekly* would give a lurid account of the Burnsbrookers' bad spirit. Other local sheets, jealous of Ironwood Village, would reprint Clairton's account.

Jim was grateful for Laurie's tact in not asking what he planned to do now. His mind and heart were full of just one overwhelming feeling—of frustration. He had hoped for so much for so long that the disaster closed over his head as the sea does over a man who can't swim. Yet underneath every wave of anger, he refused to drown. He remained that much himself.

There was little talk on the back seat, either, and Jim was surprised how soon he turned into the home lane. Dick Anderson's car followed and pulled up alongside. Then Laurie asked, "Do you think the umpire was blind—on purpose?"

Jim shook his head. "No, he called other close ones right. It was hard to see at that distance."

"But *twice!*" Jean put in. "I can't forgive him for doing it to Roy *twice.*"

Jim said nothing. It was done, over with—and no use getting heated over it again for nothing. Dick Anderson opened the car door and said to Laurie, "One jump'll do it, Sis." Then, turning to Jim, "I'll call you in the morning."

"Thanks," Jim said. There was nothing like breeding, like tact so long practiced that it became part of you. Dick could be as understanding as his sister.

The Wayland car arrived, and Tony said, "I'm taking Goat and Garry home for supper. Be seeing you."

Jim nodded, again thankful for Tony's understanding. "You home tonight?"

Tony nodded. "Any time you say."

"About eight then."

Jim drove to the barn. He neded to be alone. Once more, the milking would calm him down, give him time to think.

The cattle were glad to have him there as the thunder piled down on the roof. He was glad to be with warm living beings that could not talk, couldn't ask him what he was going to do—even though he knew. He had never given up yet on any project that his heart had warmed to. He was as done with Winnow and the other two as if they'd been struck by lightning. But that did not end the team.

Jim was deeply concerned about Frank, who had been so utterly disgusted. He might balk at going through all that effort for the few weeks of summer remaining. It was too early to milk, so Jim lay back on a pile of sweet-smelling hay to think. The drumming of the rain faded and stopped. Little by little, Jim resumed being the stanch self he customarily was. Presently, Frank Lafferty came in.

"So this is your hideout," he said and sat down by his ace catcher. "What're you going to do now, Jim?"

"Milk and get a bath."

"You know what I mean."

"And you ought to know me by now." Jim sat up. "This time we'll *build* a team, instead of throwing it together."

Frank patted Jim's knee. "I knew you'd say that. . . . I knew it. We'll do that very thing."

7

James Antaeus McNail

JIM AWOKE to unaccustomed gloom. It was raining. The thunderstorm had been merely the protruding front of a spell of weather. The full weight of yesterday's calamity fell upon the boy's waking consciousness. He was a leader with nothing to lead. His brag to Frank that he would *build* a baseball team to last sounded empty. In this gray dawn, with water dripping from eaves and leaves, his unrested mind refused a new ambition. He hated to face his friends and Ike Morse. He felt like lying where he was until his family had left the breakfast table, but he pushed his legs out of bed in scorn of that feebleness—and almost trod on Bogie.

"Get up, you slug-a-bed!" he ordered. Bogie rose and yawned, with each leg stretched to a different point of the compass.

As so often, being his true self brought unforeseen reward. His family greeted him as if they'd never heard of Clairton, and Jean, who always brought a book to meals, looked up from the page and said, "Good morning, James Antaeus McNail."

"Now what've I done to deserve that?" Jim looked at his really attractive sister and thought he was lucky in his family.

"Don't you know who Antaeus was?" Jean felt sure that she had him cornered.

"I soon will," Jim retorted with his first smile since the previous afternoon.

Jean ignored that insult. "Antaeus was a big wrestler, and every time anyone downed him and he touched earth, he rose stronger than before."

Although Jim got Jean's meaning, he asked, "But what happened to his clothes?"

"Oh, you!" Jean was slightly exasperated. "I was paying you a compliment."

"It sounded like a farm ad," Scott put in.

"Do give the girl a chance!" their father exclaimed. "Jim can do with a few compliments."

"So go ahead, compliment me." Jim grinned. Somehow his spirits had righted. His family was a defense against anything.

"You've had it, you nuthead," Scott said. "All you have to do now is to get up—stronger."

"Jim got up last afternoon," Uncle Frank said to Scott, then he turned to Jim. "When do we have a get-together, Anty?"

The family laughed at that—Jim with them, but Jean's compliment had sunk in.

"What about now, Frank? As soon as I've conquered these, that is," Jim answered. The "these" was a pile of hot cakes. He reached for the maple syrup of his own making. "My middle name's *Homemade*, if anybody should ask. You can't buy a breakfast like this."

"Or such satisfactory people to eat it with," Mrs. McNail said with warm pride.

Her husband rose. "It's lucky these sweets you all throw around don't fatten us or we'd weigh a ton. Go ahead and have your bull session. You might clean out the bullpen at the same time. By the way, Jim, how did they ever come to call the baseball dugout a bullpen?"

Jean saved Jim from answering that embarrassing question by closing her book with a bang. "Why don't they ever mention a woman in their serious books? It's always a man does this, or thinks that, or says the other."

"Now what?" Scott inquired.

Jean opened the book again. "Here it says 'a man is most miserable when he thinks he has no power over circumstances.' Why not a woman? Why shouldn't a woman be most miserable when she thinks she has no power over circumstances?"

"Because there never was such a woman." Scott grinned at his unusual powers of fancy.

"Maybe you're right," Jean agreed unexpectedly, and left the dining room with her dishes.

The four males at the table laughed and Frank said, "Jean's got something, Antaeus. Come to think of it, no woman ever concedes that she has no power over circumstances."

"Not if the circumstances are men," Scott said. "I—"

A knock on the door interrupted and, to Jim's utter surprise, Dick Anderson came in with raindrops glistening on his fair hair.

Mrs. McNail, who liked this city boy with the excellent manners, urged, "Sit down, Dick, and help Jim finish these hot cakes. Scott, get a towel. Someday maybe I'll find out why boys never wear hats."

"Because they've swelled heads and can't find any to fit." Jean had somehow learned that Dick had arrived and could not stay away. Jim noticed the delight in her eyes and woke to a new fact of life: Jean wasn't just his kid sister any longer. She was a young-young woman, with charm in every contour and a new outlook on life. He must have a mind like a medicine-dropper not to have noticed this before.

Dick dutifully mopped his head and attacked the hot cakes. Between swallows, he said, "I bet you have the Burnsbrookers' future all doped out, Jim, and I want to hear it—but first I have to get a crazy request from Laurie off my chest. You know, when you showed her the barn, how she squalled out, 'What a place for a life-size game of hide-and-seek!' Well, she has a dozen kids in her day-school group, and she sent me here to see if it would hurt the barn if she brought them out this morning or afternoon."

"Pop's in the kitchen," Jim told him. "I'll ask him. When do you have to go back?"

"I don't have to. I can phone Laurie anytime before nine, and there won't be any business at the Lake in this rain."

"Then hold everything," and he vanished from the room. To have Laurie there, perhaps to help her run the show, would be just dandy, he had promptly decided—and he began planning to pray for a lot of rainy days.

He returned to the dining room in two minutes. "One *yes* and fifteen cautions," he announced with a grin. "I'll talk to her." He went out to the telephone in the hall on that errand.

He had hardly finished delivering the ten-minute message and rejoined Dick, who had only two hot cakes to go, when there was a racket of machinery in the yard which stirred Bogie to remonstrances. Jean popped her head through the doorway to ask, "Did anyone send for the Fire Department?"

Jim looked out the window and answered, "It's Garry Steep and another guy on a motorcycle." He went out to invite the pair in. They used the towel, took off slickers, and Mrs. McNail offered to make more cakes. The boys said they had jobs and couldn't stay.

Garry introduced his gaunt, red-haired friend as Chuck Young, and explained that the latter had seen the Clairton game. "You tell it," Garry said to Chuck.

"Well, I liked the way you fellows played," he said to Jim. "It was your win and you got short-changed out of it. Garry said you'd want replacements for Winnow, Lowbridge, and Gresham, or you'd fooled him all your life."

Jim looked at Frank, who nodded slightly, for he had been impressed by Garry, and birds of a feather do usually run together. Jim said, "You guessed it. Those three guys are out. That means we need a first and second baseman and center fielder. We've got subs but we're out for the best players. Frank is planning to get the team together tomorrow evening. Can you come here a little before seven?"

The visitors could and Garry asked, "Do you know Rod Kregill, Jim? He's kind of tough, but in the right ways."

They laughed and Jim said, "Bring him along. If we had two teams for practices, we'd learn faster."

That settled, Garry and Chuck exploded off on their cycle.

By now, Jim's earlier mood had done a turnabout. The sun had come out on his affairs; he was his own man again.

There was still more light to come. When Laurie arrived with two big cars full of excited small children, and a couple of attractive girls for helpers in watching over them, she brought a copy of *The Village News*, fresh from the press. "There," she pointed triumphantly to a column on the first page, "I could love that man!"

The man was Isaac Morse, who had written a column which Jim read with growing emotion. It gave a realistic description of the game, with just estimates of the playing of both teams, but it was the final paragraph that lifted Jim's feeling to a new high. It ran:

> There was no excuse for what followed. The umpire called wrong, but he was far from the play. Unfortunately, he had called wrong once before. We must and do believe that both mistakes were unintentional. The fatal mistake was the inexcusable conduct of three Burnsbrookers whose pugnacity brought on the fight that ended the game, and I trust ended these players' connection with a promising team. There was wild talk last night that this team was done, that no other teams in the Valley would want to play such a trigger-happy nine. But these talkers do not know Jim McNail who created The Burnsbrookers and Frank Lafferty who coached them into fair shape in a remarkably short time. Jim is a sticker, and we predict that a far finer team will emerge from this seeming catastrophe. What is more, this office phoned to three Valley teams, two of which had had representatives at the Clairton game, and all three said they would be happy to play the Burnsbrookers this summer. What is more, a good friend of this newspaper, an ex-professional umpire, has offered his services free for the next game or two that the Burnsbrookers play. He saw the game at Clairton, because he can no more stay away from a game than a bull can pass up a red shirt. This paper will publish Captain Jim's plans when available.

Jim was inwardly thankful that he had not divulged his bruised spirits of the evening before. He had earned the confidence that Frank and Ike Morse and the fellows had in him. Never again, he promised himself, would he despair.

Perhaps Jean was right in giving him that wrestler's name. He would not fail to live up to the original Antaeus. He would be knocked down, no doubt. But nothing in this world was going to keep him from getting up again, either.

Laurie, coming back from the kitchen, where she had gone to greet Jim's mother, saw the lights on his face. Being a girl, she may have suspected that some of the light came from her presence there. But she only said. "So many people have faith in you, Jim, it must do something for you."

"It does . . . it does everything. And this piece of Ike's is a real shot in the arm. Thanks for bringing it."

Something in his voice warned her, and she said quickly, "Now I must hurry to the barn and see that my brats don't tear it down. Your father is very good to let us use it."

"Frank, Dick and I are going to hold a council of war," Jim said, "but it won't last all morning and maybe we can do something to make the going easier. Scott and Jean and I have spent a lot of wet days playing in that barn."

The screen door slammed—and if some of the light did go out of his face, it went only as far as his heart. He noticed a ray of sunlight slanting through the clouds and said under his breath, "Get back in again, if you want. I don't need you."

8

The Battle of Pebble Creek

As THE EVENINGS of practice re-soldered the broken team, Jim began to realize that the savage disappointment at Clairton had carried unforeseen benefits with it. The new members, Rod Kregill and Chuck Young, were keener players than Winnow and Lowbridge. Garry Steep also added an element of appreciation that pleased Uncle Frank. He appreciated being one of the team and appreciated Frank's coaching. Even before it had played a game, Jim felt that the new team was more of a unit than the old one, with its subtly discordant members.

"I've seen you two playing somewhere," Frank said to Garry and Chuck at the first practice. "I wonder where."

"Wherever you were looking," Chuck answered with a grin. "We never stop."

"Likely at the Village picnic," Garry added. "We filled in for the old men who dropped dead from the heat."

"Mercy! Are you serious?" Mrs. McNail put in.

"Pay no attention to him," Rod Kregill advised. "He means the men were a little tired."

"I remember now," Frank said to Chuck. "You stopped a red-hot liner out in left field and beat the batter to first with it—as clean a throw as I ever saw this side the pros."

"The runner was old," Chuck said modestly. "A cow could've beat him."

"I hope we're not wasting you at second base," Frank said.

These three recruits were only one of the dividends of the Clairton fiasco. Pebble Creek, a rival of Clairton, asked for a game, offering a choice of dates. Frank advised Jim to accept for the Saturday a fortnight off, so that the teamwork could be as smooth as possible.

This day came in hot, but not muggy, and Ike Morse had written enough about the contest to insure a grandstandful of rooters for the Burnsbrookers.

The batting order, after considerable nail-chewing, as Frank put it, stood as follows:

Dick Anderson, right field
Rod Kregill, 1st base
Jim McNail, catcher
Roy Mason, 3rd base
Sam Slant, left field
Garry Steep, center field
Henry (Goat) Edwards, shortstop
Chuck Young, 2nd base
Tony Wayland, pitcher

and Joe Chapman, Belt Burrows, and Rink Davis, subs.

As the team sat on the bench, waiting for Pebble Creek's signal to start, Dick Anderson asked Rod Kregill a question that had long puzzled the Philadelphian. "Why all the warfare between Ironwood Village and Ironwood School?"

The dark-haired son of a Polish immigrant answered, "It's mostly talk, Dick."

"Even so, I don't get it." Dick mopped his neck. "The

School gives steady employment to the Village and the students don't bother the Villagers—to hear my sister tell it, anyway. Yet you might suppose they were sworn enemies."

"Could it be the natural envy of the middling poor for the lucky rich?" Chuck Young put in.

"Maybe, to some extent," Garry agreed. "The small car owner casting eyes at the big car owner."

"Not to mention the distances they come. Some of the students travel in jets, and they're off to California or Florida for Christmas, while we're saving up for a trip to Philly." Chuck let out a faked sigh and everyone laughed.

"Worse than that, the School is always talked up big," Rod Kregill added. "Big shot lecturers and players and millionaires are coming to shoot off their mouths or visit their kids."

"They can have it," Goat declared. "I'd rather be free. They have about fifty rules a day to keep them tied up proper. And when they do crum over to the Village to buy smokes or sneak a beer, and get caught, we're blamed for letting them have it."

"Just the same, we know the School's the biggest thing we've got," Rod said. "Mr. Ironwood's a really big man. If the School caught fire, you'd see what we really thought of it. We'd break our necks to help put it out."

"Human nature's not exactly logical," Tony Wayland said, "like umpires."

The others laughed. Just then, Laurie Anderson came over to speak to her brother, and the benchful of young daters looked at her approvingly. The month she had spent outdoors with the youngsters at the Day Camp had given her a most becoming sun-tan. The story of daily happiness was written on her mouth, in her eyes, in her laugh. Jim felt the fox of envy gnawing at his otherwise robustly happy heart, for Ted Everson had brought her to the game in his car—and would take her home for the weekend. This Dick had told him. Dick was secretly pulling for Jim. He was far too cagey to say so out loud.

"My, you look stunning in that uniform," Laurie said to the bench in general.

"We have Ike Morse to thank for that," Jim told her. "He took up a collection for it, and there was money enough left over to buy all the balls, bats, and other equipment we'll need for a year."

"Did he choose the color?"

"You did," Jim told her. "Remember at Clairton, when we were talking uniform, and you wanted it plain blue with white lettering? When Ike Morse asked me, I relayed your and Jean's opinions."

The summons to start play interrupted their conversation. The crowd quieted. Pebble Creek was a small name for a lot of big-spirited people. The baseball grounds supplied one long grandstand, loaded with kids, their parents and uncles, with a sprinkling of grandfathers. Frank said, "I like places that keep their old names, instead of calling themselves New Pittsburgh or some such nonsense. This will be a hearty game."

Dick Anderson led off. He found himself puzzled by the Pebble Creek pitcher, who took hardly any stretch but, having sunk the ball in his glove, held it a moment at his belt line and then threw. The first pitch was a fast one that barely clipped the corner. Dick, in his nervous eagerness for action, reached for it, as Frank had told him fifty times not to do, and caught just enough of it to produce a high foul. The catcher, running like a sprung hare, got under it at the right time and place and Dick was out.

Rod Kregill looked the seasoned player. He was big for eighteen and the roomy uniform's gray-blue bagginess increased his size. He waited watchfully. The ball curved in to make it a strike. The second pitch had little on it and Roy pounded the ball out and up for a large loop that had not quite the momentum to evade the deep center. Rod returned to the bench.

"Stay loose and you'll have him," Frank said to Jim as he walked out into the blinding spot on which a thousand eyes were focused. He forgot that Laurie was looking, forgot that he was captain and must play the part, forgot himself. But he could not forget what a dozen years of Frank's training had planted in every cell of his mind and body. His eye caught the ball as it left the pitcher's hand, followed it in, signaled play to his body. The bat struck the ball squarely and was flung aside, his legs pistoned him to first. The left fielder was still racing for the ball. Jim headed for second. The fielder leaned over, scooped the ball up, threw. Jim slid. The umpire signaled safe. Roy Mason headed for the plate.

"Bring him in, boy," Sam Slant called.

The pitcher looked at second, looked at third to warn the baseman to be ready, and threw a fast one at knee level. Roy stood as if mesmerized, while the umpire called "Str-r-*rike!*" Jim walked back to second.

On the next pitch, Roy singled safely between first and second and Jim stood at third. Sam Slant was up, and, in no time at all, he was struck out by a surprise curve, a surprise sinker, and a simple fast one so surprisingly rapid that he never saw it. He returned to the bench with a surprised look on his face. "That guy's smooth," he said. "I'm sorry, Frank."

Jim and Mason came in for their gloves and Frank said, "You've proven that the pitcher can be hit. Now let's get these fellows out, one, two, three."

Tony Wayland took his throws and fooled the first Pebble Creeker with a curve, another curve, and still another curve, when, by all rights, he should have varied the diet.

"Tony's got Scotch from playing with Jim," Frank said to Belt Burrows. "He likes to save."

Tony's pitch to Batter 2 was a vicious ball, inside and very low indeed, but the umpire called it a strike.

"Generous man!" Rink Davis confided to Belt. "If that ball was as high as the batter's kneecap, I'm a mud turtle."

Tony returned to the curve for a second strike, and then bushed the batter with a precise duplicate.

"They're sensible guys!" Chapman said to Frank. "They just don't believe a pitcher has such a one-track mind."

Tony then retired the side with a set of change-ups, just when the batters were expecting three of a kind.

Goat slapped Tony's back on the way in and said, "You're a deceitful cuss. When did your mamma stop believing you?"

Garry Steep was up and Jim counted on his good nerve. Nothing flustered him. On the other hand, it took him a little while to accustom himself to a new pitcher. He now let the first pitch pass—a strike. The second pitch fooled him into fouling, but at least a foul beyond any player's reach, although both the catcher and third baseman ran for it and just avoided a collision.

Garry did connect with the third pitch and drove it along the grass at comet speed, but the pitcher saved by a spectacular lunge and a left-hand throw to first at ground level, beating Garry by inches.

"That play'd look good in the World Series," Frank observed.

"Smart fielders all of them," Roy Mason said.

Goat Edwards' middle name was spunk. His very walk to the plate proclaimed it. Rink Davis laughed, and Frank said to him, "None of that's put on. Short guys have to swagger some."

"I'll say," Tony concurred. "Goat's solid courage—and they'll be finding it out soon."

Goat's first demonstration of independence was given by the simple act of waiting. He let the first pitch pass—a ball; and the second, also a ball; and the third, too low. If the pitcher expected Goat to gamble on the fourth being a ball, he was fooled. Goat put every one of his hundred and thirty pounds into the hit which almost nipped off the pitcher's right ear. The center fielder ran up to it and got it to first fast, but Goat was already there.

Then came one of the pretty plays of the afternoon—from the Pebble Creek standpoint. Chuck Young rifled a fast grounder inside third base. The shortstop scooped it up and whirled it, in an accurate toss from knee-level to the second baseman who tagged the incoming Goat, without any ifs or buts, and then managed to throw to first before Chuck reached the bag.

"You have to admire clean work like that," Frank said. "Our boys have nothing to blame themselves for."

The Burnsbrookers fought on, inning by inning, and in the fifth, sixth, and seventh had two men on base, only to fail to score. Pebble Creek did no better, although once they had loaded the bases, with their best slugger coming up. Tony Wayland merely pitched better and got the man out in four tosses. Both teams were eager to play the tie out, although the continued strain had fatigued them.

The eighth inning changed the story. Jim was up and drilled through center for one base. Roy Mason placed the third pitch far out on the left-field line and Jim reached second. Sam Slant had two strikes on him before lofting a foul, an easy catch for the third baseman. Then Garry

Steep hit a two-bagger deep between center and right field, enabling Jim to score. Goat Edwards brought Mason home with a second two-bagger that the center fielder muffed, but sent in fast enough when he got his hand on it. Then Chuck Young hit far out into right field but was caught.

The mounting tension of the long afternoon's deadlock now stilled the crowd. Pebble Creek was in real trouble. They needed three runs to win, and they hadn't managed to get one man home all day.

Jim walked with Tony to the mound to refresh the pitcher's memory on what the first three Pebble Creekers had done. "Your low one close inside slaughtered the redhead," Jim said. "The gawky gink who's next up fouled because he reached too far for your outside corner pitch. The third guy waited too long."

On the bench, Dick Anderson was saying, "Tony's scarcely thrown a pitch above the waist all day."

"His fast one's a natural sinker," Frank declared. "It's always doing something."

"When he does pitch high, it rises," Goat said.

They stopped talking, for the first Pebble Creeker, the redhead, was slowly waving his bat, like an angry tomcat's tail. Tony hurled his winning low and inside ball, but the redhead must have been remembering, too, for he met it with a crack that sent shivers down Jim's spine. The ball overpassed the left fielder, but he managed to get it to third to prevent a home run.

"That Sam's some humdinger!" Belt Burrows exclaimed.

Tony may have been jogged a bit, or his fingers may have slid over the crease—he himself did not know what happened—but the batter slugged the ball just over the shortstop's head and again just out of reach of Sam Slant at left field. The result: one run for Pebble Creek, one man on second, and none out.

Jim walked out to Tony and asked, "Do you want to walk the next guy? He mayn't wait this time, and the two after him aren't much."

"I'd rather strike him out," Tony said.

"I hoped you'd rather," Jim told him.

Tony then proceeded to strike out the waiter in three vicious pitches, each one as low as the law allowed and at express speed. The Burnsbrook bench applauded.

Then Tony struck out the next batter in four pitches, one throw being a ball by half an inch. "*Tsch, tsch!* Can't have that!" Rink Davis said. "Imagine taking four throws when three does it!"

"You ought to be drawing cartoons," Frank told him. "With that sense of humor, you'd go places."

On Tony's first pitch to the next and crucial batter, his toehold was less than firm and he hit the batter. Luckily, the Creeker ducked in time to avoid the full blow and could take his base.

The next batter up was the Pebble Creek captain, the drive-in man, the shot-putting type with heavy shoulders, who had been trying for wallops all afternoon, usually overreaching himself. "Keep them low," Jim signaled, and Tony nodded. He looked at the bases, reared back and let fly, and it *was* low. But the captain caught the ball at full swing at the extreme top of the swing and sent it scudding off in the direction of New York State. The Burnsbrookers had to watch in mute anguish as the Creekers journeyed around the bases. Then the field flocked in.

Tony's jaws were clenched, trying to conquer his feelings. Jim walked in with him and said, "You did just as I told you to."

"Not quite," Tony said.

The Pebble Creek team bunched and yelled for Burnsbrook. The captain came over and shook hands with Jim,

"A good clean game," he said. "Let's have another before Labor Day."

"Right," Jim agreed. "We had baseball today."

"I hear this is the first time you've played together," the captain said.

"We have three new players, but we can't make an alibi out of that." Jim's voice was steadier now. "You beat us, but don't count on doing it again."

The ride home was so different from last time that Jim was far from being totally unhappy about it. And when they all stopped at the Farm and filled up on Mrs. McNail's sit-on-the-grass supper—fried chicken, lima beans, new corn, plenty of gravy and hot biscuits, with iced tea and apple pie with ice cream on top, the team was anything but depressed.

Frank Lafferty summed it up before they separated. "You men played well. If there's such a thing as a winning loss, you had it. You lost the count but you won experience and confidence and took the long strain in your stride. You felt like a team to me, not just a bunch of ballplayers."

They all parted in a haze of good feelings, and only then did Jim feel the strain. Suddenly, he was dog-tired—but happy-tired. And the ride home with Laurie beside him had added a new sort of confidence. She was Ted Everson's girl, but the summer was young yet and he'd show her some baseball and as much attention as the law allowed.

He was in his pajamas when there was a knock on the door. He called a response and Jean stuck her head inside his room, said, "Good night, Antaeus," and ducked out.

It was nice to have a kid sister like that, Jim thought as he got into bed. He was a lucky guy all round.

9

Three-ring James

As JULY gave way to August, Manager McNail shed his energies in all directions.

Helping his father was his first duty. The farm was producing with all its might in a stream of plenty that must not be wasted. In addition, Jim had thrice-weekly practices with his team, with *The Village News* keeping a close tab on its progress.

In mid-July, the Burnsbrookers had played Swiftwater, in the foothills of the Poconos, for a satisfying 4 to 1 victory. In the last week of July, they had forged ahead of the Pinetree Pirates, 3 to 2, when a semi-cloudburst intervened on the Pirates' behalf in the sixth inning.

Now Jim was looking forward to a return engagement with Pebble Creek on Labor Day. His team had been knit together by competition and burned to down the Creekers.

Yet Jim was hardly happy, for Ted Everson still clearly had the inside track with Laurie Anderson. They had the rich life of Ironwood in common, and Ted, as Jim had to admit, was not only an exceptionally good ballplayer but well-off financially and blessed with a magnetic personality. Further, he fully appreciated this charming, active, and self-possessed girl.

Sometimes Jim wished that he had his brother's easy way with girls. Scott shamed him on the Romeo circuit. He wasn't fussy, and if a girl he was dating became an encumbrance, he shifted his affections to the next one as easily as one turns off a spigot.

"It's lucky girls don't go in for mail-order weapons," Jim said. "You'd have died long ago."

Scott laughed. "If you were a maple, you'd keep all your last year's leaves. Me, I'm a bear for education."

Jim smiled at the picture of a tree holding onto its lifetime of leaves, but having felt the sunshine of Laurie's smile, he was no more able to forget her than to forget his own name. In his easier moments, he knew he had much on which to base his hope of Laurie's attention. She was deeply feminine and conscious of another's feelings toward her. She had felt a real sympathy for him in his disappointment at being unable to attend Ironwood School. She admired his growing ability to act as catcher-manager of his team. And no girl could be oblivious of Jim's person; his farm-built body had a natural ease and health, while his face was firming with the manhood in him. Laurie knew character when she saw it. Compared with her brother Dick, who was about Jim's age, Jim was a young man, while Dick was still a boy.

Jean McNail was called Pry-eyes by her brother Scott, and with reason. Her endless reading had prepped her on the adult world, and she had not read fifty love stories for nothing. She interpreted Jim's attendance on Laurie with unusual accuracy, as was the case in the matter of the honey.

One pleasant summer evening, he had dressed up in the hope of taking Laurie out on the Lake, since Ted Everson had late-evening duty. Jean observed the clean shirt, clean dungarees, and that he had scrubbed his hands for ten minutes. He had wrapped up a box of honey, donated by his bees. Jean noticed, later in the evening, that her brother brought back the honey, and, with "womanly intuition," connected it with some disappointment for Jim at Laurie's hands.

Jean felt indignant without knowing all the facts. The schedules for workers at the Lake had been changed on August first, freeing Ted for the evening in question, and he had taken Laurie to a drive-in movie thirty miles away. She had not known of Jim's call or the honey. Nothing was as bad as Jean pictured.

However, no girl of fifteen could forgo assisting at a love affair. Jean's way was to quote the experts, the novelists. So the very next morning at breakfast she supplied her brother with a quotation, she supposed tactfully. "I just read something I'm going to remember, Jim, because it reminds me of you."

Jim was pouring honey on his waffles and barely heard his sister. She grew impatient, since she so wanted to help. "Are you listening?"

"Don't I always?" he murmured and wished the honey would hurry.

" 'A passionate devotion to a course strikes a path through circumstances.' "

The honey still had Jim's attention and he said, "That's nice."

Jean was stung by his inattention. "Oh, I think you're insufferable!" She had also just acquired that adjective.

Jim still held the reluctant honey over his waffle but looked at his sister. "What've I done now?" he asked innocently.

"You know perfectly well. I'm trying to help you and you pay no attention."

"Help me?" Jim was genuinely puzzled. "How?"

"I can't *tell* you. Don't you see?"

"You mean about baseball?"

"*No!*" Jean was really indignant. "Of course I don't mean about baseball. How dumb can you be?"

Jim set the honey jar down. Somehow or other, he had stepped on Jean's feelings and he was truly sorry. "Let's begin again, Sis. I am dumb, I admit. Tell me again what you quoted."

Jean, in her turn, was quick to hear the genuineness of Jim's apology. "It was George Meredith who said it," she told him. "He knew a lot about unsuccessful lovers. He was trying to encourage one when he said, 'A passionate devotion to a course strikes a path through circumstances.' "

Jim's mind could strike a path through considerable obscurity when he really brought it to bear, but now he replied, "That's just what we Burnsbrookers are trying to do, Sis. Did Mr. Meredith mention the time element? It takes time to make a team. . . ."

"Oh, you!" Jean's frustration was getting her again. "George Meredith wasn't talking about baseball. He probably never heard of it. He was talking about love and *I'm* talking about honey. Honey keeps, Antaeus McNail."

Illumination suddenly bathed Jim's mind in its strong glow. The thwarted dater hardly knew whether to be sore or amused or touched by his sister's interest in his relations with Laurie. She saved him the need of replying by hurrying out into the kitchen, and Frank Lafferty came in with instructions about spraying the lower orchard for the last time.

After he finished briefing Jim, he said, "I've been telling Tony to relax more. You and all the boys ought to take it easier between swipes. The infield particularly needs to let go between innings and when they're on the bench."

"I know we've got to stay loose, but getting that way's hard."

"Not if you practice it. Nobody thinks he can bat or run or throw without practice, and easing off takes just as much drill. When you sit down, slump, go soft. Feel like a jellyfish. Then the habit'll soon take over. Only practice makes habit and only habit makes ease, and only ease makes you master. There's no short cut, unless you call thinking a short cut. Think about it when you shower and when you get in bed at night."

"Maybe we should have drills in relaxing. I'll add it to the list."

Jim had kept lists ever since he was made responsible for certain farm chores. Scott kidded him about these lists and wrote out a specimen list for his morning: "Remember to get up. . . . Don't forget to dress. . . . Go downstairs. . . . Be sure to swallow food at breakfast." Jim had laughed and kept on penciling down the daily duties.

Now, as manager, he found the list-keeping habit a help in ridding his mind of details. By the morning of Labor Day he had a list as long as Bogie's hind leg. Now, with the team arriving, he checked off items he could so easily have forgotten: *Sponge* (which was to put in his catcher's mitt if the Pebble Creek pitcher banged them in too hard). *Extra pencil* (for scorebook, no one yet had invented an unlosable pencil). Look over first-aid equipment—and so on.

Mr. and Mrs. McNail came out to see the team off. "My, you look nice in those uniforms!" Mrs. McNail said. "Who did them up for you?"

"Laurie got them done at the school laundry," Dick Anderson told her.

Jim glanced at Laurie with admiration as well as gratitude. She knew how to meet praise easily, completely without self-consciousness. He knew that ability came with "class," as the Village called it. He was aware that the boys' admiration of her was magnified because she was able to appreciate it without seeming to notice it. Queens learned this art, but how did democratic girls make it part of their bearing? He, himself, was unduly conscious of the boys' envy of him when Laurie got out of the car that Dick Anderson was driving and stepped up into Jim's mongrel vehicle.

Labor had drawn a perfect day for its celebration. There was not a great deal of talk when the Burnsbrookers reached the scene of their previous defeat, the Pebble Creek diamond.

"They've got the same ump, I'm glad to see," Tony said.

"But also the same pitcher," Goat remarked. "I kind of hoped to hear he'd fallen and broken his neck—not severely, of course!"

Frank Lafferty had rearranged the batting order. Dick Anderson had improved less with practice than anyone else. This bothered Jim more than he liked to admit, even to himself. Dick was the apple of Laurie's eye, and when he was at bat or fielding, she judged him more with her heart than with the almost professional acuteness with which she judged the other players. Frank knew that it was essential to have as many men on base as possible before the strong hitters came to bat. He again suggested to Jim that he retire Anderson to the bench and bring Rink Davis to the line-up, but Jim said, "We owe the Andersons a lot, Frank. I think we can win as we are, and it's the last game of the season. I don't want Dick chewing the hurt over through the winter."

Frank knew that that was not the whole explanation,

but he gave in. He moved Chuck Young up and put Dick eighth in his place. The line-up now read:

Chuck Young, 2nd base
Rod Kregill, 1st base
Jim McNail, catcher
Roy Mason, 3rd base
Sam Slant, left field
Garry Steep, center field
Goat Edwards, shortstop
Dick Anderson, right field
Tony Wayland, pitcher
subs: Rink Davis, Joe Chapman, Belt Burrows.

Chuck Young at the plate looked like a bird dog, Jim thought—a bird dog at the point. Chuck did everything but sniff the air. He was poised, held his bat motionless, lost no phase of the pitcher's motion. The first pitch was a mistake on Pebble Creek's part—straight and innocent. Chuck smashed it for a stinging drive—into the pitcher's mitt. But the impact or the surprise was too great. He not only dropped the ball but nudged it with his left toe in the act of picking it up. It rolled, his reach edged him off balance, and his throw to first was a step wide. Thanks to this complicated lack of design, Chuck was safe.

"Well begun *isn't* half done," Jim cautioned as the laughs died down and Rod Kregill went to bat.

"Show him your thumper," Rink Davis yelled to Rod.

But the Pebble pitcher had made a resolution: no more innocent pitches. Rod hit over the first, under the second, and nipped the third for a foul, up and back, and the catcher squeezed it for an out.

Jim dropped the second bat, his loosener-up, and faced the foe. "Patience does it," he had kept telling his team. He had broken himself of going after bad balls. He had also stopped planning for a two-bagger. It had proved for him as fatal to think too far ahead of yourself as not to think. The ball was the thing—and here it came—wide.

What a letdown! Jim's impulse was to make the pitcher pay for the slight slump. The second pitch grazed his arm as he stepped back, but the umpire contented himself with calling it ball two.

Now, Jim thought. He didn't want to walk. He wanted to hit. He studied every instant of the Creeker's delivery and, instead of stepping out for a fierce swing at the treacherous ball, he waited that fiftieth of a second and connected just the right distance up the sphere, a shade over center, and drove it into the blue distance, pushing Chuck home and landing on third. The applause from his bench and the large crowd from Ironwood Village sounded remote. Success was living two lives at once, making one doubly alive. He tried to haul himself down to earth, the safer place.

Roy Mason was up and knew what to do. Frank considered him the steadiest, most dependable player of them all. Roy gave out confidence. Jim had come to feel that this player could come through with what was needed. This time, a hit would do it. The pitcher put one over with a nasty curve. Roy waited. One strike. The pitcher repeated and again Roy waited. Strike two. The pitcher smoothed out his wind-up, which was as good as advertising something else, and else it was, a trifle high. Roy hit down on it viciously and burned up the atmosphere toward right field. Jim came home. Roy stayed safe at first. Sam Slant's long, slim figure stood in a rather stoop-shouldered question mark beside the plate.

"The guy's shell-shocked," Rink Davis remarked about the Pebble pitcher.

It was the wrong diagnosis, however. The pitcher was in reality just settling down. He threw one so fast that Goat declared it left a trail of sparks like a shooting star. One strike. Then he threw a curve. "I've seen horseshoes with less curve than that," Belt said. Two strikes. The next ball was this pitcher's first slider. It slid under Sam's stick, and Garry Steep took his place.

Garry had a wide-legged stance, which Goat described as a stubborn mule's. Frank Lafferty had tried to pull his legs together, but Garry said it gave him a solid feeling. Too solid, Frank complained, because he started to run awkwardly. This made all the difference in Garry's first smack. It grounded to the Pebble shortstop, who tossed it to second as a greeting to Roy.

"So far, good," Frank said as Jim's men took the field.

"So far should've been farther," grumbled Belt.

Rink asked Frank about the balk rule, saying, "I don't think their pitcher minds it very much."

"The pitcher must bring his motion to a full stop for one second with a man or men on base," Frank said. "But few umpires carry stop watches. Maybe the guy does shave it short, but it's a very fine point, and I don't feel like raising that point now."

Tony took his throws and felt good and loose, and he had an arsenal of pitches. As Goat had remarked at a practice, "Tony makes wisecracks with his arm." He did indeed tease the batter with humiliating change-ups. He now opened the bombardment with a ball so fast that the batter simply didn't see it, and following it was a ball so slow that the batter didn't wait for it. Tony's third throw clipped the inside corner at a good pace and the batter, edging back a little so that it wouldn't sandpaper him, lost his timing again.

The second Creeker fared no better, failed to touch leather.

The third fouled up and down into Jim's mitt.

"One of our time wasters," Goat shrugged on the way in. "It must've taken two minutes."

"Stop cracking wise and hit," Frank told him.

"He makes me dizzy," Goat said. "All legs, spikes, elbows and flying hair. Let's get the ump to order a haircut."

"Get out there," Frank ordered. "They're in a bind and we've got to make it tighter."

Goat, as cocky as he was short, said something to the umpire that made him smile.

"The risks he takes!" complained Rink.

"Goats are butters," Tony said. "Instead of the pitcher working him, he'll work the pitcher."

However, it wasn't that easy. Goat connected with the second pitch—but almost into the first baseman's pocket. Dick Anderson did less, making fast passages through the air with his bat but hitting nothing. Tony Wayland was plugged on the left arm by an erratic ball.

Instantly, the Burnsbrookers were on their feet. But the Pebble Creeker ran over to Tony, en route to first, and apologized most sincerely. He was truly embarrassed. Tony rubbed his biceps and said that it was only a glancing hit. Jim came back to the bench with the news that Tony wasn't hurt and that the Creek pitcher was genuinely sunk by the bad throw. He was not so upset, however, as to forget his art, and he struck out Chuck Young with three blazing pitches.

The game had developed into a pitchers' duel. Four innings gave no further runs. Then Pebble Creek began to creep ahead. There is a rhythm in games that has its way. In the sixth inning, the rhythm was pro Pebble Creek. Tony worked on his control, but the first Creeker up stepped into a fast, low, and seemingly perfect pitch and knocked it into the sky tantalizingly between center and left field. Sam Slant and Garry Steep both called, each thinking it surely his, and so nearly collided that the ball bobbled from Sam's mitt to the ground.

That was Sam's, Jim thought but said nothing. The game had been singularly errorless.

Tony pitched wide on purpose to the next Creeker up, for he remembered how eager this lanky boy was to hit at anything. This time, the batter did not overreach himself. Instead, to Jim's surprise, he dropped the ball for a perfect bunt, equally distant from Jim, Goat, and Tony. In the scramble, the batter reached first and the man on second slid safe at third.

This time, Jim did go out to Tony and say, "Remember, this fellow can't see a ball unless it's shoulder-high."

Tony dispatched a low, speedy ball, but the Creeker must have visited the oculist since last time up. He cracked into Tony's fast one with a swing so professionally measured that the ball headed toward the Great Lakes for a homer. The Pebble Creek crowd hoisted cheers to the calm sky, and now the score read *Burnsbrook 2, Pebble Creek 3.*

In the long business of growing up, Tony had come to match Jim in being able to take adversity without being paralyzed. He said nothing, just went ahead and systematically struck the side out.

The Pebble Creek population was now mad with enthusiasm, hope, determination, and plain delight. The rhythm had reached the end of its swing, however—and stayed there. The game was stalemated until the seventh inning began with Burnsbrook at bat. Jim's boys gathered about him. They had learned that he was indeed their leader in a pinch. Even Frank Lafferty yielded to their confidence in the steadiness of his big young friend and stayed in the advisory background.

Jim said, "Get loose. It's all done by attention to one

play at a time. We can beat these fellows at hitting, running, stealing, pitching–"

"–and catching," Goat put in. The others nodded agreement. "So, if we can do all that, why bother to play?" Goat had to add to be Goat. His teammates laughed and went loose.

Burnsbrook went to bat with the head of the line-up. On the first pitch, Chuck Young whipped a ground ball past the pitcher into center field territory for a safe hit. Rod Kregill had learned much from previous visits to the plate and he got all the wood on the ball on pitch number three. He reached first and stopped. Chuck had passed second but returned after a couple of strides, for the ball was cleanly fielded.

Jim, third up, fought back his natural nervousness and smashed a level-flying ball far enough into center field to get him to first base. With Kregill at second and Chuck at third, Roy Mason looked solemn as he faced the pitcher.

That young man had a determined chin. He took pains to give Roy nothing easy. Roy's sweeping swing started off a grounder that took a crazy hop and struck the shortstop on the shoulder, then bounced far enough away to cross up the Creek hopes. Chuck, already halfway home, slid in for the tying run. The shortstop's throw to the catcher was somewhat wide, and the catcher was late in reaching third with it. Sam Slant stepped into the box.

The Creek pitcher conferred with the catcher–and then struck Sam out. Steep went to bat. The pitcher erroneously supposed that this guy was some sort of knickknack, easily dusted off and put back on the shelf. He threw, but his toe slipped, which resulted in a slower ball. Steep stepped into it, hit with the nose of his hard-colliding bat, and before the dust of the runners settled, the score had changed to *Burnsbrook 5, Pebble Creek 3.*

But that halted the Burnsbrook scoring. There began a breathless period of taut ball. Tony Wayland reached a real height. To see him on the mound, nobody would have guessed that he had an ounce of pressure on him. He threw ten balls . . . and that was the game.

The teams parted in good feeling and the Pebble Creek captain said to Jim, "We'll get back at you next summer."

"That's a promise," Jim told him. In the exhilaration of the moment, a similar next summer existed in his dreams. He thrust out of his mind all the contingencies that made a repetition of this summer look impossible. He was happy, his fellow players were happy, and he planned an evening that would make him even happier–if it came off.

10

On the Lake

During the ride home, Jim asked Laurie, so quietly that the celebrators on the back seat could not hear, to stay after the team left the Farm and go canoeing with him.

Laurie hesitated long enough to hold the knife-edge of fear to his hope, then said, "I'd love to, Jim, but I must be back at the School before ten, you know. That's rules."

"In *summer?*"

"You know that's just being sensible. The School is responsible for us. Our families wouldn't let us come otherwise."

"You might suppose morals were regulated by the clock!" Jim exclaimed thoughtlessly. Success had gone to his head a bit.

Laurie laughed. "It's reputations, Jim. Mr. Ironwood is always quoting about the necessity of avoiding the appearance of laxness. He says that blueprints and patterns come first. He says that if you have the pattern of maturity in front of you, it's easier to be mature."

Jim had to admit that there was something in this. Laurie

went on, "After all, Mr. Ironwood is a pretty good example. Think what that school has done for thousands of boys and girls in his twenty-five years of running it."

"When is a person mature?" Jim asked impatiently.

"Mr. Ironwood has an answer for that, too. He says an individual is at least approaching maturity when he has established order in himself."

Jim thought that over a moment. "Pretty good," he finally assented. "Pop has established order in himself, and we recognize it. So has Mom, in her own way."

"I think you have, too, Jim," Laurie said quietly. "Today couldn't have happened if you hadn't had it and so been able to help others have it."

Unfortunately, just then, the low conversation was interrupted from the rear. But there was the hour on the Lake ahead, Jim solaced himself with that thought. He felt good, with the day's victory in his pocket and the responsibility of the team off his back. He felt tingly in body and spirit—and could hardly have told where his body left off and his spirit began!

Mrs. McNail had another fine buffet meal ready for the team. . . . Before the players separated, Jim said, "You heard me promise Pebble Creek a return game next summer. I've thought a good deal about our team and I want to think some more before I talk about it. We're going to keep on, somehow."

What with the glow of victory, the good food, hearty comradeship, and personal plans for the rest of the evening, the Burnsbrookers shouted their agreement—and then hurried away. Jim told Dick Anderson that he would see Laurie safely to her door, and presently she was sitting facing him while he quietly paddled the McNail canoe out into the Lake.

The weather had been good to baseball players that day,

and now it outdid itself for the boys and girls in canoes on the unfrequented lakes in the vicinity. The breeze had become merely a drift of cool air when Laurie and Jim started out. The shores soon faded into shadow, and presently Jim let the canoe drift so that he could concentrate on his companion. Suddenly, she asked, "Do you really think that you can revive the Burnsbrookers next summer, Jim?"

"I won't need to," he answered to her surprise. "They won't need reviving, for I'm going to keep them alive."

"Through the winter?" Laurie's voice rose unduly.

"When they hear the plan Tony and Frank and I have doped out, they'll keep fit through the winter. They all ski or play basketball and wrestle, and during the Easter holidays we'll train in Florida, like the Phillies."

"You do look ahead! But who puts up the money for the trip?" Laurie leaned forward in her eagerness to hear his plans.

"We've got cars enough to take the crowd. We can camp out in Clearwater, where the Phillies train. We can probably find part-time jobs. Uncle Frank used to know—and still knows—some fellows on the Phillies' payroll. We can watch them train. Please don't say a word about this to anyone Laurie, not even to Dick."

"I won't," she promised with a laugh. "Nobody'd believe me. I like people to think big, Jim."

"Ironwood started me thinking this," he told her. "When I heard that I couldn't take an extra year there, couldn't play on the baseball team, I was good and sunk, believe me. Then I thought that the next best thing was to *play* them. I know they're the champions of this region and we're just a pick-up team, but we'd play Pebble Creek and Cedarlane and Hinsdale and perhaps even Cliffside first. Pop's always talking objectives—there's your pattern again. Well, if we had Ironwood School as our great objective, I think we'd—we'd, well, we'd outdo ourselves—and, I guess, have a lot of fun in the bargain."

"I think you're wonderful," Laurie said quietly, and Jim thrilled at the words because they were obviously sincere.

"Well, I have a lot of incentive, as you can guess," he said, also quietly. He wanted to say more, much more, but now was not the time.

"How do you expect me to keep your plans bottled up in me all winter?" Laurie asked, to steer the talk away from the too personal.

"You can always talk to me about it," Jim retorted.

"Have you a match?"

"No woodsman was ever without a match. What do you want to set fire to? The lake, the canoe, or me?"

"I have to see my watch. I think it must be perilously near ten."

The beam of his flashlight proved that it was, and he ruefully headed the canoe for the distant Ironwood School dock.

After seeing Laurie safely to the door of her quarters and paddling quietly back to the McNail boat shed, he was glad to have time to think the day over. The way to find out things was to work, or be alone, or enjoy such happiness as filled him now. Nothing had ended with the summer, not even the Burnsbrookers, and as for his friendship with Laurie—that, he felt, was just beginning. Maybe someday before long Ted Everson would find this out.

11

An Obstacle Race Months Long

School opened. Burnsbrook Farm was put to bed for the winter. The great massacre—of turkeys, naturally—was celebrated with double Thanksgiving by the McNail dynasty because the price of turkey meat stayed high.

Christmas approached. Jim presented Laurie with a large box of Jim-made maple sugar, hidden in a large box of Jim-cut Christmas greens. Laurie presented Jim with a new book on baseball management entitled *A Run for Your Money* and illustrated by photographs of illustrious players. In the front she had written, "A Merry Christmas to Manager Jim with best wishes for the Burnsbrookers' New Year."

The New Year came in with a road-piling blizzard. The opening of school was delayed three days, which pleased Scott and Jean and helped Jim with some free labor. He was enjoying his school-free days and being paid farmhand wages.

Mr. McNail kidded Scott and Jean with, "Fine Scots you are! The more money you lose by not going to school, the happier you are."

"We're saving gas and teacher's temper," Scott said. "How's that losing money?"

"Knowledge is power, power is money, and you look out the window and wish it would snow until May."

"We haven't spent a cent in days," Jean joined in the give-and-take. "That makes us Scots again, according to the stories."

"Or un-American, anyway," Scott declared. "Yesterday you said we didn't like money, or we wouldn't get rid of it so quickly."

"I said, 'Waste not, want not,' and that goes for words," his father countered. "Let's get water to the chickens."

Washington's Birthday brought warm air from the south. Jim made lists of things to be done in preparation for the trip to Florida. . . . March arrived. . . . The week of departure arrived. . . . Two days before departure arrived —and Frank Lafferty went to bed with a temperature of 103°! Dr. Baines arrived and said that it looked like pneumonia. Frank sent word downstairs to Jim that he was to carry on with the trip, just as if his Uncle Frank sat behind the wheel. He was to take the Lafferty car as planned and find some older person to go along.

Supper was a quiet meal, with Frank's place empty for the first time the McNail family could remember. Jim was still telephoning to the team members, telling them the unhappy news about Uncle Frank and asking for suggestions about a last-minute substitute.

"Say *Jim* and you get *jam*," Scott said quietly.

"But Jim always equals jam," Jean countered. "Jim beats every jam he gets into."

"But I wish he'd get the breaks for once." This was the hidden Scott coming to view in an emergency.

Mrs. McNail brought in the teapot and said to her husband, "The boys simply must have an older person along,

Bruce. I know they are responsible in lots of ways, but there are certain emergencies that even they would not know how to meet." Mrs. McNail looked at her husband earnestly. "I hope you'll dissuade Jim from this undertaking until Frank is better, if he can't get some older person to take Frank's place."

"The boys can't put it off, Mother," Mr. McNail told her. "Of course, Jim's middle name is reliability, and the boys respect him, but I agree that they should have a man along. I wish I could get away myself. But don't worry, we'll find somebody."

Just then, Jim came dashing into the room, a broad smile on his face. He was so excited he could hardly speak. Finally, he managed to share his news with his eager family. He had received a telephone call from Isaac Morse. The reporter had heard about Uncle Frank's illness and the hunt for another man to go to Florida with the boys. He had been planning a trip down there himself, to pick up some first-hand material for his sports column in *The Village News*, so he thought he might as well go a little sooner than he had expected and take on a group of youthful sportsmen for traveling companions, the Burnsbrookers. The Florida trip was assured—and on time!

Two mornings later in the frosty dawn, the good-bys were brief. A honk from a car indicated that Tony Wayland had arrived. He was taking Roy Mason, Goat Edwards, and Joe Chapman in his car.

"Have a good time, boys, and don't swallow any grapefruit whole," Mr. McNail called.

"If in jail, write," Jean said happily.

Mrs. McNail embraced her oldest child and said, "Do be careful, Jim. And remember that one of you boys is to telephone home every evening, so word can be passed around to the rest of the parents involved as to how things are progressing—and where quick contact could be made in both directions, in the event of an emergency."

"We will," Jim promised once more, knowing how much this would mean to their parents—and also how sensible it was.

Scott said, "I'll keep Bogie happy. I'll let him sleep on your best suit every night."

"Where is my dog?" Jim exclaimed. He hadn't seen his friend for a good ten minutes. He looked in Uncle Frank's car and found Bogie on the floor in the rear, trying to be invisible. The retriever's air of wistful yearning wrenched Jim's feelings, but he had to tell Bogie to get out. The dog obeyed at the slowest possible rate. His master patted him, told him to be good and obey Scott—and drove away fast.

By the time he had picked up the two subs, Rink Davis and Belt Burrows, his whole team had assembled inside Ike Morse's office. The sports editor was writing down their names to finish off his column for the next day. He said, "I've alerted the neighborhood. We all have an interest in the Burnsbrookers, so you fellows must come back rich in skill."

Jim, Tony, and Rod Kregill were the drivers, with Dick Anderson making the fourth when they reached Philadelphia. Isaac Morse would ride as a passenger—unless he was needed as a driver.

Jim said, "We'll surely get separated during the days on the road, so I've written down the route to take all the way. We'll meet at Dick Anderson's home first. If anyone has an accident, wire me there. If I have one, I'll wire Tony there."

"Is it a race?" Rod Kregill asked.

"Naturally." Garry Steep grinned.

"There are speed laws in each state," Jim said. "And cops. Our object is to play ball."

The others knew what he meant.

At the first stop, Dick Anderson's home—an apartment on Philadelphia's Rittenhouse Square—they would redistribute passengers. The three cars had kept together pretty well on the way, and the reporter and the eleven young men were invited up to the Anderson apartment for coffee and doughnuts. Jim knew that the travelers were rarin' to go, but he had to meet Laurie—and her parents—while he had the opportunity. The beautifully furnished rooms seemed hardly lived-in to him, but the Andersons' reception of him and his team couldn't have been warmer, he thought, if they had lived in a home.

Mr. Anderson, tall, and graying already, looked Jim over so carefully that the boy felt that Laurie must have had a hand in this inspection. "I like the way you stick at things," her father said. "Laurie has told me about your disappointments. I've learned, as you may be learning already, that every obstacle you overcome gives you confidence and confirms your purpose. I've met what I consider a successful man, now and then, and, in every case, the secret of his success is his refusal to be diverted from his purpose."

"Jim's purpose is to be on his way, Dad," Laurie said. "Jim, how are we ever going to hear? Dick has never written as much as a postal in his life."

"Oh, no?" Dick laughed.

"It depends on who's being written to, I gather," Mrs. Anderson said, and the rest of them laughed at Dick.

Jim quietly explained their nightly communication plan and Mrs. Anderson said that she would telephone his parents for the progress reports.

As Jim had foreseen, when the four cars headed south, they soon separated. Rod Kregill, carrying Garry Steep and Joe Chapman, slid out of sight first, with Rod shouting, "See you at dinnertime." Tony Wayland, with Roy Mason and Goat Edwards, vanished next.

"Go ahead," Dick Anderson said to Jim. "The garage is bringing my wagon around. We'll catch up." So Jim, with Isaac Morse, Rink Davis and Sam Slant, pulled out, leaving Chuck Young and Belt Burrows standing with Dick on the sidewalk.

"We could've got into three cars," Rink said.

"Not with the tent, thirteen sleeping-bags, cooking outfit, extra clothes, and bats. Nobody could move," Jim reminded him.

"We're driving nonstop, aren't we?" Sam asked.

"Have to keep up with Hot-Rod Kregill," Jim told him. "Each of us can drive till he begins to tire. Rink and you can toss for who's next. But we will all meet for dinner at the places indicated on the route maps I've given you. They're well-known chain restaurants. Anyone can telegraph or telephone me there in case of a breakdown—and we can phone that promised word home. Final meeting place is the Clearwater post office—and don't forget to keep an eye peeled for good camping places as you enter the town. We want to locate as near the Phillies' training grounds as possible."

It was not Kregill, however, who met Jim and Co. in the Clearwater post office, just fifty-one hours later. Tony Wayland, Roy Mason, and Goat Edwards were sitting in their parked car, sharing a local newspaper.

"You stop to pick cotton?" Tony asked with a grin. He looked at his wrist watch. "We've been here one hour, six minutes and eleven seconds."

Just then, to Jim's considerable relief, Rod Kregill drew up. Garry Steep called out, "We're ahead of Dick by one red light." In a moment, Dick pulled in.

"How about camp sites?" Jim asked the huddle. "We didn't see any likely spots in the last five miles."

Goat Edwards said, "We found a honey of a place about three miles back, but the owner was as haughty as an ostrich and said, '*No camping*. Can't you read?' I said we were from Pennsylvania and didn't need to read since television came in. And he said, 'Nobody is allowed to camp within thirty miles of Clearwater.' Then he pointed out the sign we were supposed to see, and it was signed by their Chamber of Commerce."

Jim's spirits faded. He was hungry, tired, dusty, sleepy. For half the length of Florida, he had been looking forward to setting up their long, open-face tent by a stream, under some trees, and he was stymied at the start.

Tony was talking now. "We didn't believe old sour-face and I called up the Chamber of Commerce. It's all too true."

Jim's stubbornness stirred, for in his book no manager was ever stumped. "Let's get washed up and eat. We've got a baker's dozen brains to pool on this." Although he did not express it out loud, he appreciated the way Ike Morse had let the boys manage everything for themselves on this trip.

"There's a diner around the corner," Tony said. "When guys have to wait as long as we waited, we had time to find out a lot. We needn't have brought the tent, for it won't rain. The Chamber of Commerce won't let it. Also, we found out the way to the Phillies' grounds. Also, we bought a paper for the help wanted ads."

"You're sure on the ball," Jim said. "Let's eat while we study the ads."

"We've studied them," Tony told him. "We've marked a dozen possibilities."

Jim said, "We can't afford *not* to camp and we certainly

can't go back thirty-five miles to camp, so we've got to get permission from someone to camp on his private grounds. I don't suppose the Chamber of Commerce can stop that. We can trade work for the privilege."

They devoured a huge meal and prospects looked brighter, but after they had consulted the want ads and had telephoned to half a dozen places, the outlook became grim. No one needed twelve boys—or any fraction thereof. One florist wanted a delivery boy. "That wouldn't be so good," Belt said. "Even if the man was willing to take on a different boy each day, it wouldn't help our practice."

"Let's go see him," Jim suggested. "He might want helpers where he grows the flowers, or at least know of someone who does. We just can't stay here and throw dimes into the phone."

So they trailed out to the florist, who, luckily, had a sense of humor when the team crowded into his shop. Ike Morse stayed out in Uncle Frank's car.

"I wish I could sell enough to employ you," the florist said. "I do want a permanent helper."

"Can you suggest some sort of employer who'd let us sleep on his premises?" Jim asked. "And we'd like to be as near the Phillies as possible."

"I ought to know someone," the man answered. "I came here from New Jersey thirty-odd years ago. Now, wait a moment."

The man vanished into an inside office. . . . The moment became minutes and the minutes dragged unbearably. "I wonder if the Chamber of Commerce controls boats," Jim said. "Maybe we could find a boat to camp on. If we—"

The florist returned, looking pleased. "You're fixed if you don't mind work and have an extra seat in one of your cars?"

"Most of us live on farms," Jim said, "and we have an extra seat. What's the job?"

"I just remembered that my wife's mother has been talking of getting her property drained. That means ditch-digging. It means keeping an eye out for snakes. But it gets you a camp site. And my son's been planning a trip north. If you have room for him, my wife will pay for the ride by supplying you with desserts. She bakes pies to help out."

It sounded fine and looked better than it sounded. The florist's mother-in-law had been born in Pittsburgh, Pennsylvania, and was not only glad to find so much skilled labor at her door but offered fair hourly wages, in addition to a place to sleep and cook. Also, she had no prejudices toward Negroes.

As soon as Isaac Morse saw that the boys were in such good hands, he left them for a hotel room in town.

The Burnsbrookers spent the rest of the afternoon settling in, getting briefed on the draining job, and cooking supper. A youngster arrived with four pies of different sorts. The boys' spirits rose to normal and above.

After leaving everything shipshape, they drove out to the Phillies' grounds to present a note from Frank Lafferty to a friend of his who used to coach for the Club. "He might not be there any more," Uncle Frank had said, "but at least it may remind somebody of me and show that you aren't out there just for curiosity."

The layout of the grounds was larger than Jim had pictured. The terrain was flat as a table, with baseball diamonds, barrackslike houses, bullpens, and offices all protected by an enormous fence. The boys, now squeezed into three cars, stopped at the main gate. Jim showed his letter to the guard and waited with the tension growing in him again.

"Never heard of him," the guard said. "If he was with the Club, it was before I came, all of nine years ago."

"Who does he want?" asked a young fellow, about Jim's age.

"Casey Cooper," the guard answered. "Ever hear of him?"

The boy shook his head but looked at the newcomers with interest. "You're not wanting to play here, I hope. Recruits've been leaving every day."

Jim told his story and why they had come to Florida. The boy broke in with, "I've heard of those schools. I'm from Trenton, New Jersey."

Rod Kregill had been looking at the boy's uniform. "You a bat boy?" he asked. And when the boy nodded, Rod said, "You're the first bat boy I've ever got near enough to talk to. Do you really get to travel all over—out to the Coast?"

"I do, because my dad's a relief pitcher. Most bat boys just work the home grounds. Look, I can take one of you in to talk to Dad. He might know where that player you want to see is."

"Can I take one friend?" Jim asked.

"That okay, Ketch?" the boy asked the guard. "These guys are going to be cash customers for ten days."

"Only two," the guard said. "And bring 'em back here yourself, or the doc'll be treating you for shell-shock."

"Okay, Ketch, and don't fill them up with your usual chowder."

"We call him Ketch for short because his Polish name is about three inches long, and he was a catcher with the Giants," explained the bat boy, who also told Jim and Tony that his nickname was Lemons because he gave out best in a squeeze. "Ketch is glad to tell you all about his big days with the Giants. According to Ketch, they were named after him, the Giants were. He's also quite frank about how he could agitate an umpire when the decision didn't suit him. The only bad feature is that he has drained himself dry of his stories but still keeps giving us the evening edition and the night extra, and so forth. What do you call your team?"

Jim explained why they had chosen *The Burnsbrookers* and he also told Lemons about the Ironwood School and why he particularly wanted to be able to play Ironwood. The bat boy was interested and exclaimed, "Now isn't that something! You tell Pop that and he won't think you're a news-nose or a gimme-your-wad guy or any of the clubhouse bugs who want their pictures taken with the big shots. They hang onto a club like bloodsuckers and you can't pry 'em off." They had reached the office by now, and Lemons said, "Let me talk to Pop first. He's the busy kind, even on a plane, but he'll let me talk."

So Jim and Tony waited and Tony said, "It's just like a hanging, only they haven't tied the noose around our necks yet. I don't like suspense much."

Jim nodded. "It sure takes a lot of wind-up to get us throwing."

"But you find out how decent most people are," Tony reminded his catcher. "That florist could have saved himself a peck of bother by just brushing us off. And Lemons here needn't have offered to help."

Just then, the bat boy came out to them, looking a little doubtful. "Pop's awful busy, but he said to ask you exactly what you wanted, and I'll tell him."

Jim stated once more why the team had come south, why they wanted to watch practice games and hear what the coaches said.

When Lemons vanished once more, Tony said, "Everything's like that obstacle race in the track meet. Can't *anything* be done without crawling through pipes and pushing through hedges? It's like having a barbed-wire fence in every doorway. I'd like something just plain open and easy to get at, for once."

"I complained about the same thing in farming to Pop once," Jim said, "and he told me plain sailing would bore us to desperation after one afternoon. He said the more opposition, the sweeter the victory."

"Just *once!*" Tony exclaimed. "That's all I'm asking. Just once let's go ahead without having to butt the opposition down."

"Well, we've had it," Jim countered. "We've had your 'just once.' We all got to Florida without one blowout or accident or anybody getting crabby even."

Again Lemons came out of the office and he wasn't smiling. "Pop isn't feeling particularly good today. He says you can pay admission to the games like anybody else and if you bother the coaches, you'll be shown out on your ear."

"Just *once!*" Tony said to Jim.

"What's he saying?" Lemons asked.

Jim explained, "He means he'd like the breaks, just once, without having to bust his neck against a stone wall."

"His neck looks all right to me," Lemons said. "And I was coming to the breaks. I like you guys wanting to beat that school you've looked at all your life. Now they mostly let me do what I please here when they don't notice. . . . I've got it! You come in those uniforms you brought along and everyone'll think you're paid rookies from one of the minors and won't ask any questions. I'll keep an eye out for you and, when I'm not working, I can take you two, anyway, to the bullpens and other places where they're really sweating. Tell your friends not to stick their heads into the clubhouse or talk to the players and you'll see whatever you like. Look, I'll take you to the stands now and show you where to sit, so I'll know where to find you."

Jim looked at Tony, "You asked for the breaks just once," he said, "and now you've had it." Then he turned to Lemons, "My Pop is the real Scot, and since I was a kid, he's been telling me to take nothing for nothing, because the bill, when it comes—and it always comes—might be bigger than I can pay. So now what can we do for you?"

The boy stiffened. "I didn't ask anything, did I?"

"No, but we've got to do something in return. That's only fair." Jim tried to explain his seeming rudeness.

"Okay, send me the news when you beat that pants-pressed school," Lemons told him shortly.

Belatedly, Jim saw that he was talking to a real guy. He said with quiet sincerity, "Thank you, Lemons. We've got a newspaper rooting for us. In fact, their sports writer pinch-hit for our sick coach so we could get down here. We'll send you all the write-ups."

When they returned to the gate, Lemons laughed. The boys were standing in a semicircle and listening to the guard hard. "Good old Ketch!" the bat boy exclaimed. "It's a big day for him when he can find a new ear, and here he's got a dozen."

Dick Anderson said to Jim, "We thought you'd gone back North. Anything doing?"

"Low and inside," Tony replied for Jim.

The next eight days were crammed with activities. Isaac Morse kept in touch with the boys, but he did not hover over them. A few times, he treated them all to a bang-up dinner, feeling that pie, no matter how good, provided a lop-sided diet.

As for the desired insight into the making of professional ballplayers, Lemons had lots of time on his hands and he enjoyed being appreciated. He was unused to being treated as an equal, let alone a fount of wisdom in the baseball world. Nor had he ever known fellows like this bunch of princes from Ironwood Village. He took particularly to Goat Edwards, a brother wise-cracker, and to Jim.

The work of draining their hostess' grounds proved heavy and tedious for the boys. Jim found it best to divide his dozen into squads, since there weren't enough tools to go around. Consequently, they watched the pros at work in small groups. They found an extra dividend in having Lemons watch *them* work. He knew as much baseball as a keen book, and took a great deal of pride in being able to chew them out like a professional coach. He loved the importance of ordering someone else around. Thanks to the uniform the Burnsbrookers wore on his advice, they were unmolested by officials. The only place they were forbidden to penetrate was the players' private quarters.

In return, the visitors took Lemons swimming with them by moonlight in the Gulf waters. "Ironwood Lake never gets this warm in the hottest summers," Tony said. "Does it come to a boil here in July?"

"I've never been here then," Lemons told him. "But there's one thing you can say about ballplayers—they're clean. I always used to think soap was a dirty word until I saw these athletes use it. Always showering. I wonder they don't grow fins."

The high spots came on game days. The Burnsbrookers watched the Phillies play the Minnesota Twins the day after they arrived. Three days later, they played the Chicago White Sox, and the next day the Pittsburgh Pirates. Two days after that the Phillies beat the Detroit Tigers. Thanks to Lemons, the young observers squeezed a lot of value from these games, because he played them over later, discussing the pitcher's work, the catcher's direction, showing how the shortstop messed up one double play and saved one, explaining errors, calling attention to sharp plays.

One day, Lemons induced his father to watch Tony pitch on one of the distant diamonds that was not in use. This authority was a man of few words and he didn't care to repeat them. "Remember that hand when you throw," was his first piece of advice to Tony. "It's too much out in the open. If the batter sees the way you wrap your fingers around the ball, he's nearer to guessing what's coming."

Tony tried to follow directions and got the nod of approval. "Forget your fast ball when you're in trouble and bank on your curve. The first two innings are the hardest on your control. After that, you should be loose and forget your nervousness. It helps to count ten between pitches. Better still, say the alphabet up to J—if you know it. Some of our guys obviously don't. Try it now."

Tony found that doing this did divert his mind a little from the strain of showing off before a critic. Then Lemons' father said, "Most beginning pitchers count on the *next* pitch to make good. That's foolish. It's the pitch you're making that matters. Put everything on that."

Frank Lafferty had mentioned this often unrealized fact, but Tony had forgotten it. His current coach went on, "About every fourth fast one you pour in has a habit of rising. Keep it down. Also, keep it out of the middle. You can't offer a juicier invitation to smash out a homer than a fast one through the middle at the height the batter likes. Keep every one down—down—down. *Think* down."

Jim was listening, memorizing on the side. These points were hardly new but they gained emphasis coming from this sturdy, forthright man. "As a general rule, you'll find it pays to throw wide to left-handers and close to right-handers. Now I want to see some action." He turned suddenly to Jim. "Bring in your batters—your best."

"They're all best at times," Jim said, to save any hard feelings, because he was going to call Roy Mason up first.

When Roy came to the plate, Tony was told to pitch a different ball each time, and to put it through all the channels. After each pitch, the coach commented on it and on Roy's reaction. Presently, the other batters were run through the mill. Lemons' father had come to say a few words—he spent two hours with his pupils.

At the end, he said to Jim, "You've got the makings of a clean-up squad. Remember what I've said and practice it tomorrow. Practice is to your game what digestion is to your body. Nothing's much account until it's digested and working for you. Skill can become effortless only through habit. Habit is a kind of bat boy. It always hands you the right play—if you've practiced."

"Tell Jim what you told me about being a manager," Lemons urged his father.

"Well, the thing is not to *over*manage. You've been taught well by that Uncle Frank of yours. A catcher is the team's eyes, as you know. If he's got memory, that's a third eye."

"But when does managing become overmanaging?" Jim asked.

"When they think you're fussy. When the heat comes up through the collar. Every player is entitled to one error in a game—so don't chew him up for it. But not two. Pull him out if he makes two, and rest him. And remember this, however much you're worrying underneath, you must appear confident on top."

"That's easier said than put over," Jim countered.

"Not if you're *sure*. Be sure inside, and positive outside. Smile once an inning, and praise someone. The secret of able management is self-management."

"How long did it take you?" Jim asked.

"I'm not halfway up the ladder yet. When I started, my boss said, 'You've got to learn to be a good actor. Don't show your feelings. It never hurts to keep your men guessing.' 'And how do you do that?' I asked him. 'If you have to ask, you ought to give up managing,' he said. 'It's easy—be gruff and pleasant, be firm and easygoing, be sour and sentimental. See?' An actor can change his face, that's all."

Jim felt out of his depth. "I never put on an act in my life."

"That's what you think. I've been watching. You've set up each batter to come to the plate by some word that made him feel good, yet you've not grown windy. The boys obviously like you and trust you and will work for you. That's being a manager. Now I've got to go, but maybe I can dig up a team of rookies for you to play. I want to see Tony here in action. Maybe I'll see somebody we can use in a year or so. I was a scout before I put on the uniform. Remember, a uniform's not just clothes. It's a reminder you're part of a team and owe your best to it."

"I don't know how we can ever pay you back for all this," Jim said, and the team made enthusiastic noises that meant the same thing.

"That's easy. Beat that school you've told my boy about—and let me know."

The next few days—far too few for all that they offered—were full of what Goat Edwards called "compressed work." He could have called it "compressed joy" as well. The woman the boys toiled for with pick and shovel knew a good thing when she saw it and she began to feed them well—much more than pie.

Lemons' father was as good as his word, and assembled a rookie team which rubbed the visitors' faces pretty thoroughly in the Florida dirt on the last afternoon of their stay. But their coach, umpire, and encourager praised them for their occasional sharp play and for their spirit. When it was over, the boys knew that they had gained immensely. Nor were all their memories of sweat and weary muscles.

As a thank you for Lemons' father, the boys had induced their employer to sew up a flag of the right colors and enclosed a simple note with it: "Our thanks for everything, and a pennant to your team, sir." All twelve signed this crisp but heartfelt missive.

The moon had arranged to throw its light on the Gulf waters and, following the game, the dozen Northerners lazed in a before-bed refresher in the tepid softness.

"There's just one thing missing," Dick Anderson commented.

"Yes, alligators, sharks, sea-serpents, and that nice blob of jellyfish that stings you to death," Goat said.

"He means girls, idiot," Tony explained. "That reminds me, Dick. Have you written to Laurie yet?"

"No, I sublet that privilege to our manager." He nodded toward Jim in the yellow dusk.

"For how much?" asked Goat—and got the expected laugh.

"I'll let you read the contract when you can see better."

Jim said nothing. He was not entirely happy about Dick's confident high spirits for a long-threatening reason. Rink Davis's playing had improved faster than that of anyone on the team. It was his right to have a permanent berth with the Burnsbrookers. This meant demoting the weakest player, and it was obvious to all but Dick by now who that player was—the brother of Jim's dream girl.

Just as one mosquito can ruin a bedroom, this unfortunate fact had prevented the Florida trip from being completely perfect for Captain McNail. He kept shoving any decision out of his mind for the future to handle.

From a reclining position in the Gulf of Mexico, Rink Davis stared up into a milky sky and noticed a ring around the moon. "Up home, that'd mean a storm," he said to Tony Wayland.

"Here it means a red face to the Chamber of Commerce." Tony laughed as a wavelet washed his face.

"Three days from now, we'll be wearing snow shovels," Roy Mason said.

12

The Blow Falls

BEFORE THE BOYS went to bed, Jim turned on the radio in Frank's car, to see if the moon had offered the right prediction. The weather forecaster said, "The deepening low pressure area over the Gulf States will cause heavy rain. This disturbance is moving in a north-northeast direction and will be followed by much colder weather tomorrow."

"Maybe we'll have to buy that snow shovel," Jim said. "How much money do we have left, Tony?"

"Nearly sixty bucks," Tony answered sleepily. "That's got to feed us and buy gas, remember."

Manager Jim divided their bankroll by twelve. If they drove fast and had no repairs, they could have two meals a day. He had come to one conclusion—they must keep together this time.

This they all were glad to do. The feeling of solidarity had strengthened during the rush of experiences. They were not only a baseball team on the diamond but a tightly knit bunch of friends. Working together had done much for them. Distance from home had done something, too. But Jim McNail's quick detection of the signs of possible animosity had prevented any real breaks in the underlying harmony. Also, the sense of having achieved the results for which they had hardly dared hope helped.

Ike Morse had been quietly proud of his young charges. He had tucked away many a memory that would make excellent copy for his column through the months ahead. For their part, the boys had long since voted him tops.

It was still raining in Georgia. South Carolina was swept by torrents of water imported from the Gulf Stream. The roads of North Carolina were waterlogged. Virginia's rainfall, as reported by radio, exceeded three inches. It was in Maryland that the battery of Frank Lafferty's car went dead. Fortunately, the party had kept together as Jim had planned. Tony drove ahead to the nearest garage and, after some argument, a new battery was installed on the roadside—and their remaining forty dollars reduced to twelve. Ike Morse's hand had instinctively gone to his wallet during the transaction—but he had wisely withdrawn it.

"From here to our Farm we lose weight," Jim said grimly. "We're going to need that snow shovel."

At Washington, D. C., they dropped off the florist's son, who had proved a good sport, traveling in Rod Kregill's car.

In Delaware, the snow took over. . . .

The Philadelphia streets were filling up. "Come in and get a square meal," Dick Anderson urged.

"We can't unload a dozen wolves on your folks at this hour," Jim told him. "Also, we'd like to get home before the roads are closed. It's snowing an inch an hour. Thanks just the same."

He had been wise, for the wind backed into the northwest and the snow started to drift. . . . He led his flotilla into the Burnsbrook Farm lane at 10 P.M. "Come in, everybody. Mom will fill us up."

"That's no reason why you should feed my gang," Tony said.

"I've another reason," Jim countered. "We won't be together again for a good while and I want to get your approval of a plan I've been working up."

Scott had plowed the lane, and the first thing Mrs. McNail said was "My, you must be hungry!"

"Just starved, ma'am!" Rod Kregill exclaimed.

"Starved nothing," Goat Edwards said. "We died of starvation two days ago."

"Then you should be fed very slightly. I read it in a book." Jean got a laugh with this.

Mr. McNail suggested, "Three teaspoonfuls of warm milk and half a soda cracker, Mother."

Sam Slant said, "It's only Goat who died. I guess the rest of us could survive what Mrs. McNail has in mind."

Mrs. McNail's mind ran to hot soup and sliced ham and mince pie, plus accessories. While they waited, Jim said, "I penciled down this note to the athletic director of Ironwood School. Maybe you can suggest improvements." Then he read: " 'Dear Sir, You may have heard of the Ironwood Village baseball team, *The Burnsbrookers*, on account of our beating Pebble Creek last fall. Since then, we have trained in Florida and hope to play several teams around here this spring. Your Saturday schedule is probably filled out, so we challenge you to a midweek game. Hoping to hear from you soon, yours very truly,' and I signed it from the team."

The reaction was quick and satisfactory. "They'll take us on," Sam Slant declared. "They can't be sewed up for all the midweek games."

Jim was pleased and the happy crowd would have talked

until dawn if the snow had not been making so fast and Scott hadn't announced that it was only five hours until milking time.

"Thanks, Mom, for everything," Jim said when the door had shut on the last departing back. "If only Uncle Frank had been along, it would have been perfect. How is he, really?"

"He's doing well. He phoned this afternoon from Atlantic City, where his married sister is putting the finishing touches to his convalescence. You call him tomorrow."

This Jim did and heard that Frank would be back in a week, so he saved the details until then.

No reply came from Ironwood School until ten days later and Jim's suspense grew. Finally, his trips to the mailbox at the lane's end were rewarded—by a brief negative. The athletic director of Ironwood School regretted to inform the manager of the Burnsbrookers that the spring schedule was complete, including midweek games.

Jim was glad that he was alone there in the cold impersonal white desert of drifted snow when he learned the verdict. He was sunk. He had been confident that his proposal for a midweek game stood an almost certain chance of acceptance. This blow recalled the previous death of his hopes when he was denied attendance at Ironwood School. He had counted with all his heart and being on this opportunity to obtain a toehold, at least, on Ironwood's diamond.

He walked slowly up the plowed lane, for he shrank from the chore of telephoning each member of the team that the big game was not to be, that the Florida trip had been in vain. Well, of course, it hadn't been entirely in vain. In fact, it had been a tremendous success. It had made such a well-knit team of them that the Burnsbrookers had a good chance of cleaning up on the best teams within a day's journey of their training lot.

This thought halted Jim outside the kitchen door. What if his team should challenge the list of teams that Ironwood School played—and beat them—and *then* challenge Ironwood? And even if their athletic director still refused, he had other approaches: Mr. Ironwood, for one, or Laurie could influence Ted Everson (so the guy had a use, after all!) and Ted could pass on the challenge to the Ironwood team, and they could demand a chance to trim this bragging Village team!

Light flooded Jim's mind and heart. First, he could put off telephoning the team until he heard from some of the teams that Ironwood played. He knew who they were, but, to make sure, he called Ironwood School and got the schedule. He spent the evening writing twelve letters.

The passing days tortured Jim with suspense, although now he had taken Tony Wayland into his confidence. Tony thought it a grand idea, whether or not Ironwood consented to play them.

Finally, replies did start to come in. The first four regretted that they could not add the Burnsbrookers to their full schedules. Then in two successive mails three schools accepted, and Cliffside was one of them! Jim had never been delirious with joy; that was alien to Scottish blood. But strong confidence was like joy. He felt sure that he was again on his way.

That evening, he telephoned to his team, explained the entire situation, and outlined what the Burnsbrookers must do before the early game, six weeks hence, with Cedarlane School.

13

"What Do You Want to Know?"

It was good to have Frank Lafferty around again. It was good to feel spring in the air. It was even good to have Scott, the scoffer, watching practice and finding it harder to offend their vanity with his teasing. But best of all, Jim knew that he had a surprise in store for Laurie when she saw them play. She could have no idea how they had improved.

Scott actually paid Jim a compliment one evening after an exceptionally good practice. "Know what? I thought to build up a team was to hunt up the heavy daters, the handsome dressers, the fast-car drivers—I mean guys with dash and all that, and you've done it with mamma's boys."

Jim laughed. "Well, I suppose our fellows had mammas, but at least they don't suck their thumbs any more. Make sense, my boy, and I'll hire you a hall."

"Don't 'my boy' me, son, or I'll tell you a thing or two about your team that'll melt your snow-capped ego."

"Then don't 'son' me or I'll call your bluff. Name one

little thing that is wrong with my outfield, infield, pitcher or catcher."

"I won't exert myself. You've got a closed mind. I couldn't open it with an ax."

Jean came into the room to set the table for supper. "What are you two fighting about now?"

"Scott has just been praising my team," Jim said.

Jean looked astonished. "Don't tell Mom. She'll take his temperature."

Scott said, "I'm trying to subdue Jim's colossal conceit before somebody else does and keep the humiliation within these four walls."

"Jim conceited?" Jean was indignant. "That's a new one."

"You weren't here. He asked me to name one little thing that is wrong with his outfield, infield, pitcher or catcher. So I will, although there are few things so unpopular as penetration. His outfield is composed of deaf mutes. It can't call the balls loud enough to avert collision. His infield suffers from overzealousness. They throw high every time. The pitcher hasn't learned yet how to break up a squeeze play, which is to pitch high and inside. Tony throws breaking stuff and ought to know it's easy to bunt a breaking pitch. Even I know that much. And as for the catcher, his peg to second is pretty good every *third* try, but it usually goes by freight."

"Don't listen to him, Jim!" Jean cried. "He's trying to get your goat."

"No, Scott is worried about my overconfidence," Jim said. "He likes to kill ants with a sledge hammer."

"Tell me what you know about this Cedarlane School you're playing next week," Scott said with barely concealed satisfaction, for he had deftly turned Jim's flank.

"You think you have me, but you don't," Jim said.

"They're playing Marston on Saturday and my scout will kill two birds with the same stone."

"See?" Jean said to Scott. "Jim thinks of everything."

However, her brother's announcement was somewhat premature. He had not actually asked Laurie yet whether she would scout the Cedarlane-Marston game. Talk about killing two birds with one throw! If she cared enough about the Burnsbrookers—and their manager—to do this useful errand, it would prove much that he wanted to know. And knowledge was always power. Indeed, if you knew what you needed to know, that was the beginning of power. His father had long ago taught him the grandpop of all questions: *What do you want to know?* It could be what do you want to know about a game, a man, a job, or about yourself. Now he wanted to know about Cedarlane and Marston—but chiefly about Laurie. Was she playing with his hopes? How did she regard his feeling for her? Or was she playing along with Ted Everson?

That evening, Jim telephoned Ironwood School at the hour when students were free to answer calls. He had thought out this conversation many times, but now, when the moment to make the request had come, he was as nervous as before an important game. Was he being sensible to ask so much so soon? How would she take it?

Laurie's voice, clear, firm, always a little eager, gave Jim the thrill he had come to expect. His physiology book had not been explicit about the nerves which a certain voice could set vibrating. Probably it wasn't physiology's job to go into that. His nervousness vanished at the sound. She seemed interested at once.

"We play Cedarlane School next Wednesday," he said.

"Yes, Dick told me, Jim."

"Have you ever scouted a game, Laurie?"

"No; it must be exciting."

"Would you be allowed to scout Cedarlane this Saturday? They're playing Marston. We need a line on both teams, and I can't get off."

A slight hesitation began to worry Jim, but finally she said, "I would be allowed to go with Dick, of course, if I had a written request from home. Dick should see the teams, anyway."

"I wish I could be that older person, but I have to be here to help move the poultry house."

Her laugh rippled over the wire. "They don't mean someone *fifteen* minutes older, Jim. But it would be fun going with you."

"We'll go other places," he said quietly. "Will you phone Dick soon and let me know?"

"Right now—if he's in. What do you want me to watch out for most?"

"Well, everything, but especially what the pitcher's got, and where each batter hits, and how good he is at running and stealing, and any signals you can catch. Perhaps I can come over on Sunday and talk it over. Is that possible?"

He wished he hadn't asked, for her voice suddenly lacked the enthusiasm she had started with, and he remembered that her free time on Sunday would naturally be claimed by Ted. However, you couldn't have everything, and he had secured a clever scout.

Thanks to the Florida practice and instruction, Frank Lafferty was happily surprised by several developments that showed up on the first day of practice. "At last you have your hands working for you," he said to the team approvingly. "Of course, baseball's a total game. Nobody ever says about a player that 'his elbow's his best friend.' In fact, you never hear much talk of elbows, except among the pros. But they are the hands' master. They keep your hands and wrists low. You can bring the glove up faster than you can drop it, and elbows order that."

Frank was surprised, too, by the improvement in the infield's fielding. "I jawed for weeks about not to wait for the hop, and now you play the ball where it is, which is right. Of course, that means you have to throw from the crouch sometimes, and I notice you're much cleaner at that." He looked at Chuck Young, playing second base, and said, "Now that you've learned to catch the ball in front of you with both hands, don't you find you keep your balance better? I think you're getting the right grip on the ball, too. That Florida air must know baseball. Somebody ought to crate it up and sell it like grapefruit."

"We lived baseball night and day," Garry Steep told him. "I never lived anything that way before."

"Oh, no?" Goat Edwards exclaimed and the boys laughed, for Garry lived with his knife and fork loyally, not to mention girls.

Tony also got a big laugh when he said, "Garry never tries to catch a girl with one hand, Frank. It's always two hands, as you say."

"If I ever said anything about girls, I take it back," Frank told them. "It would be inaccurate. They don't fit into words."

Frank was also pleased to see that Tony had learned to take a smash hit from the side. It was natural to field a ball head on, but the hit ball came so nearly instantaneously that it was safer to judge it from the side than by catching it head on. Tony had always been good at backing up an infielder, but in Florida he had learned to get farther behind the infielder.

In dozens of ways, the Burnsbrookers had boned up on the fine points, but their chief gain had been to function as a team, a machine with all parts ticking together.

When the Saturday of the Cedarlane game arrived with partly cloudy skies and a mild breeze from the south, the Burnsbrookers reached the enemy field with a new confidence.

Jim, in particular, was experiencing a sturdier hope than before any previous game, despite the disappointment that gnawed at his heart, for Laurie had failed him. Instead of scouting as arranged, she had phoned Jim in a tense voice to tell him that Ted Everson had "needed" her on the afternoon Dick had arranged to take her to the Cedarlane-Marston game.

That message, almost curt in its brevity, had plunged him into a fit of the blues comparable only with the mood resulting from his disappointment over his turn-down by Ironwood School. It had destroyed, in a few words, his expectation of a closer relationship with the girl and had deprived him of information about Cedarlane which would have been very valuable.

And Dick had apparently acquiesced easily to the change of plans and had not even gone himself. This angered Jim, who was babying Laurie's brother along on the team when, by rights, he should give his place to Rink Davis. For a few hot moments, Jim determined to retire Dick to the bench at once, but that would look like revenge, and all of Jim's training had been to deny oneself the poisonous pleasure of revenge. So Jim planned to start Dick against Cedarlane.

The little town of Cedarlane looked exceptionally neat to the invaders—and it was obviously proud of its ball team. The poplar-edged ball park had an ambitious grandstand for so small a place.

"Even those trees are ambitious," Rink said. "How're you ever going to knock a homer over them?"

"Get out your compass," Goat advised. "You don't knock homers in that direction. They'd be fouls."

"I was speaking in a general sense," Rink said, and the boys laughed, for that was Goat's excuse when he pulled a boner.

"I know this umpire," Frank said as the official in a blue jersey walked toward the plate. "He's sharp and stricter than a Sunday-school superintendent. Watch your talk. He's easily agitated by mouth fouls."

"If he's so strict, why does he allow that?" Goat asked, pointing out a comely blonde in blue jeans. "It says in the rule book, 'No blonde shall be parked in a distracting area of the ball park.' "

The team laughed, not because Goat was funny, but because of their nerves. "What's a distracting area?" Sam Slant asked, and they laughed again.

Jim was not laughing. Back in the darkest closet of his brain lay the throbbing truth that his future was coiled up in the games of the next few weeks, and now the time had come to secure that future for himself, with the help of these young men.

"Same batting order," Frank said. He had been experimenting all week and, after a cycle of changes, had returned to the line-up of last autumn—with a few exceptions: "Young . . . Kregill . . . Jim . . . Mason . . . Sam . . . Garry . . . Goat . . . Dick . . . Tony."

Jim, who had been watching the Cedarlane pitcher take his throws, thought, His arm's as limber as their poplars.

Chuck Young looked the seasoned athlete—tall without being stalky, big-shouldered, strong-armed, narrow-waisted. He would have been wasted as opener if only he could have put all that beef into the ball. Frank had labored with his stance and timing and keeping his eye on the ball, and he was able to let go. When he did connect just right, the ball started out to join the solar system.

"Easy does it now," Jim murmured, as the pitcher stood, ball in glove, waiting patiently for some inner release . . . but also to make the batter fidgety, in addition to his natural nervousness as lead-off man.

Chuck let the first pitch pass: a ball. He let the second pass: a strike. Then he surprised both teams, Frank, umpire, and attendants by laying down a bunt toward third and running like a shooting star. His rabbit gait was hardly star-like, but it was faster than it looked. Owing to a slight difference of opinion between the catcher, third baseman, and shortstop, Chuck reached first a good thirtieth of a second ahead of the ball.

"Well!" Frank exclaimed, after he'd drawn a full breath. "They'll wonder if we're fresh out of the madhouse. I'd bet my skull they never saw a game start thataway."

"Rod'll prove we're sane," Tony Wayland said.

Rod usually met expectations. The pitcher evidently intended to give him nothing that he would like. He pitched the first too low, the second rather wide, while the third brushed Rod back, almost skinning his arm. With three balls in his favor, Rod waited . . . and the next pitch was good. Rod kept his posture of concentration and waited: strike two. Jim felt the tension preventing him from swallowing. The pitcher tried a fast one on the safe side, and Jim heard the welcome sound of bat on cowhide. It was a hot grounder between shortstop and second. Chuck managed a slide into second and Rod took possession of first.

Jim was at bat next. He fought back the feeling of strain. "Attaboy!" Rod called. "Bring us in. You can do it."

Jim hit and pelted toward first, while the ball whizzed to the shortstop, who failed to hold it. Then, instead of an easy toss to third, which would have caught Chuck, this addlepate flung to first—too late. All three bases now teemed with population.

Roy Mason strolled up to the plate, apparently as easy in his mind as if he were merely going to buy a Coke. So far, Roy had never looked unnerved in a pinch. When Jim once asked him how he kept cool, Roy said, "You learn not to bother with how you keep cool if you're a Negro, Jim. You just get used to taking what comes—and it comes differently all the time. There's always a chance someone will be jeering at you, belittling you, so there's never a let-up in the uncertainty, unless you hide in the woods. What's a little old ball game to us? It's sure to be a good place all the time, because you've got an umpire to see that everyone acts fair. Never forget, it was in baseball we Negroes were first given the chance to hold our heads up in the sports field. Every Negro ought to play ball, just to get the feeling."

By now, the Cedarlanes had grown noisy, telling their pitcher to be himself and get going. But they quieted as the big Negro took his stance at bat. There was a lazy grace in the way he moved and stood that bespoke mastery —a fine sculpture of power in a blue-gray uniform.

The pitcher reared back and let go, a fast corner-cutter. From where Jim was standing, Roy seemed to overreach himself as he lunged at the tiny white sphere. The crack sounded as if the ball had exploded. It flew out . . . and then up. The left fielder's judgment was wrong. He turned and ran, then turned again and reached in a beseeching motion, which the ball ignored. On it went and the Burnsbrookers rose, shouting as Chuck came loafing in, Rod moving a shade faster, and Jim losing no time at all. Roy stopped at third, letting well enough alone. Three runs and no outs—a good time to risk nothing.

"Boy, did you hear that ball whistle?" Garry asked Rink. "I bet it's crossing Lake Erie by now."

"Let's get stubborn and not give them an out," Dick suggested.

"Sure, there'll be time for twenty homers, not to mention the small stuff," Chuck said.

Tony smiled but pointed out, "You two balloons inflate fast. They're changing pitchers."

The new pitcher came from a different breed. Sam Slant struck in vain at a curve, a slider, and an express ball, low, inside, and generally mean.

Garry Steep hit squarely—but into the pitcher's mitt.

Goat Edwards steadied the game for a moment by slamming the third pitch into the outfield for one base. But he died there as Dick Anderson's foul was an easy take for the catcher.

"Now, Tony," Frank said quietly. "Take your ten full seconds between pitches. The sun won't set for hours."

Jim had known Tony all his life but could not get used to the inner Tony, who waited somewhere in his big heart and came out only in emergencies. In ordinary life, Tony was easygoing, ever good-natured, and with a zest for life that stopped only at the outer limits of what was respectable. But on the mound he was another boy—a young man. If his temper burned, the heat turned into speed for his pitch. If the ease of his delivery suggested softness to the onlooker, Jim knew better. He usually tucked the sponge in his mitt to break the impact of Tony's throws. The pitcher's chief fault was his pressing eagerness to get on with whatever he was doing. Hence Frank's caution to count to ten.

The Cedarlane batters were unaccustomed to Tony's speed and variety. He struck out ten batters in the first four innings, with two walks, and he caught one of the walkers who had reached third by a clever steal but ventured a step too far off base. The other wilted on second.

Ironwood, however, failed to score again until the last inning of the game, which Cedarlane had limited to seven innings by agreement. Roy Mason hit a second three-bagger, but with nobody on. Sam Slant knocked him in, but failed to follow. When the Cedarlanes came up for their last chance, their coach risked everything on an experiment. He sent in three new players, and, for some psychological reason, Tony headed into a slump. Perhaps it was the natural reaction to a brilliant hour; anyway, the Cedarlane batter stepped far out to meet a wide ball and cracked out a home run. This released roars from the long-silent Cedarlane rooters.

Jim walked out to Tony and said, "If you're tired—"

"Heck no," Tony cut in. "Only a fool would have gone out to meet that pitch. The ball slipped."

"Take it easy," Jim advised. He was not worried.

But Tony's trouble had just begun. He pitched two called strikes dazzlingly fast. Then the Cedarlane pitcher, of all persons, slashed at Tony's next throw in desperation, connected, and this furious liner bounced off Tony's leg before he could get his glove down. He fell. The runner made first before Chuck Young could race in from second and gather in the ball.

Jim hurried out to Tony, who was being helped up by Dick Anderson and Roy Mason. When Frank reached Tony, he said, "You've pitched a swell game, boy. Now let Rink finish it up."

"I can do it," Tony said painfully. "Give me a minute."

"If you're right by tomorrow, you'll be doing well," Frank told him. "Rink's warming up."

In eight minutes, the game resumed, the score being 4 to 1. Jim walked with Rink to the mound. "Steady does it, boy. Take all the time you need. You've got eight helpers, you know."

"Right," Rink said. Nobody, even on the bench, knew how important this moment was to the lonely figure on the mound. Rink came from a broken home. He had waited through games and endless practices for this moment. Now it was his!

For some reason, it was suddenly hard to find Jim's glove. Rink's first pitch was wide, his second low, his third high. The Burnsbrook bench sat silent, choking back their doubts. Rink's fourth pitch was fast and fair but fooled nobody, least of all the batter, who gave it a mighty swat to left field but high. Fortunately, Sam Slant was so fleet of foot and quick of arm that he pulled it out of the air—and held it.

Burnsbrook began calling encouragement to Rink, who was already steadying down. But the fast ball he threw next had too little on it. The batter smashed a grounder between first and second, and now there were two on.

"Steady, boy," Jim said. "You'll hold this one."

And Rink almost did, but the Cedarlane batter, after two fouls, shot a streamliner over shortstop Edwards and to the left of Sam Slant in left field. The Cedarlaner on second tore through third and slid home safely. The boy on first made second but wisely stopped there.

Jim's mind was sick at this turn of things. It was doubly hard to have an almost certain victory stolen now. True, the score was still 4 to 2—but with two men on base, and Rink no doubt feeling terrible. Jim walked out to him and said, "You've steadied down a lot, Rink, and they're at the poor end of their batters. You can do this, one, two, three—but *one* at a time. Do just this one, first."

"I will, Jim," Rink replied quietly. He would do anything, anything whatever, for this McNail boy who trusted him.

Now, unexpectedly, it was Cedarlane that began to agonize. Rink pitched two clean strikes, and while the batter got a piece of the next ball, it was a foul, which Jim caught in a brilliant dashing rush, with the sun in his eyes and a stray dog at his feet. Two down, and the team scattered over the field felt less shaky and the victim of chance.

"Rink's got it," Frank said to the two subs on the bench.

"I'm still breathing," Joe Chapman asserted.

"Rink's solid underneath," Belt Burrows said.

The next pitch was a ball which might have been called a strike, but Jim kept silent. Now was no time to rile the umpire, who seemed fair. Rink's leg went up, the ball came down, brushing the batter's sleeve. Jim bit his lips as the umpire sent the batter to first.

Two on and two out. Rink, long used to hardships at home, was of an obstinate breed. The next batter struck at two fast pitches—and missed. He hit the next for a foul. He hit the next, but high, and it came down plunking into Garry Steep's glove, and the game was won! Jim ran out to Rink and pounded him on the back. Rink kept saying, "I was lucky . . ."

"You kept your nerve. You got us the game."

By now, the Burnsbrook pack was thronging about Rink. The Cedarlanes got together and gave a yell for the victors, who responded vigorously.

That ride home was a happy one for all; but their joy was shallow as compared with Jim's. At last he was one step on his way.

14

Brief Interlude

JIM'S JOY over the Cedarlane victory was overcast by Laurie's failing him. He arrived back home in time for the milking and wondered about his next move. Probably he ought to telephone her about the game, even though her brother had doubtless done so. She was free, he remembered, between seven and eight.

During the evening meal the telephone bell rang and Jean, who was as quick as a bird dog at the sound, answered it. She came back with a wide smile. "It's for you, Jim," she said. "Santa Claus."

"Santa Claus!" Scott exclaimed. "Put him to bed for six months."

At the first sound of Laurie's voice, Jim forgot his irritation. "Jim, Jim!" she cried joyfully. "I heard. Dick phoned me. I can't tell you how relieved I am. It's so splendid, and Dick said you managed the team superbly."

"His vocabulary's stretching," said Jim, who had the bad habit of treating a compliment as a sparring combatant.

"Well, I won't repeat his exact phrase." Laurie laughed. "But he meant that, Jim." Her voice lowered.

"Good." Instinctively, his voice did the same.

"Jim, I must talk to you and I can't very well here. It's too public. The booth's in the hall, totally surrounded by daters. Could you run over here and meet me at the main entrance—by twenty minutes to eight?"

"Sure thing."

"I'll be there," and she hung up.

On Jim's return to the table, Jean said, "Don't hold out on me, big child." She called him that when she felt affectionate. "I can always see when you have a secret."

"Then respect it," Mr. McNail broke in.

"Don't try to shut her off," Jim said to his father. "She might choke to death."

Scott laughed. "You're going to have an unsatisfied life, Jeanie, until Jim and I are married."

"Why do you say that?" asked Mrs. McNail, who occasionally had trouble in following her children's conversation.

"Because there's so much she won't overhear."

"I just read a book in which the little sister was a lot of help," Jean said in mock reproach.

"Fiction, no doubt." Jim laughed and the others joined him, even Jean.

"All right, all right, I won't tell you what I know," Jean retorted.

"That's a comfort," and Scott heaved a dramatic sigh.

"I declare, I never saw such a group of gallant men!" Mrs. McNail exclaimed. "Three of you picking on one defenseless little sister!"

Jean said quietly, "I'm not defenseless, Mom. I love them."

Jim thought, There's a true woman for you. But he said aloud, "You win, kid. Tell me what you know."

"I sold three more subscriptions to *The Village News*,

and when I took the money to Mr. Morse, they were talking about you and your team and Gazooks said—"

"Gazooks?" Scott broke in. "Don't be cryptic."

"He's Mr. Morse's helper. He looks like Gazooks, so I call him Gazooks. Please let me finish; it's important."

"In that case, I'll weld my jaws together."

"Gazooks said that Jim's team couldn't beat Hinsdale High. He said the Hinsdale players were really tough. He said their pitcher threw more bean balls than any team he knew and the umpires were afraid of what Hinsdale would do to them after the game. So all the close decisions were in Hinsdale's favor."

Mr. McNail interrupted his daughter. "I never heard so much nonsense in one breath. Your Gazooks creature must believe everything he hears from some blow-hard. Tell your informant to go jump in the lake."

"How did you sell those subscriptions?" Mrs. McNail asked Jean, because she did not care for this sort of talk.

"The Burnsbrookers really do it," Jean explained. "When I'm taking my turn at the stand and the customers see our sign and ask if we have some connection with the Burnsbrookers, I tell them and they're interested, so I let them know that the best way to keep up with the team is to take *The Village News*."

"I think Burnsbrook Farm should get a cut," Scott said to tease Jean, and, under cover of the new argument, he ducked out.

Laurie was waiting for Jim on the portico at the School's main entrance. She said, "You don't have to park the car. We can sit here. There's only a quarter of an hour before the bell, but I want to tell you what happened—I mean, why I couldn't scout Cedarlane with Dick. Ted Everson had invited me to a party for this coming weekend, but he had to move it up. When I told him that I'd be late because I had promised to scout Cedarlane, he said that would spoil everything, for he was going to take his guests to see the Phillies play that night and his mother was giving us early dinner. Well, since I *had* accepted for the party, and since it wasn't Ted's fault that it had been moved up, I felt I had to go. Of course, he suspected and was jealous. He's the most jealous boy I've ever dated."

"What would he say if he looked out the window now?" Jim asked, feeling much happier than he had for days.

"He'd rave," Laurie answered, "and I don't care for raving. Ted and I are good friends, Jim. We've known each other for years, and we love Ironwood and baseball and—and life, I guess. But I had to *tell* you. Writing's no good and phoning's little better."

"I knew you had a good reason, Laurie," Jim assured her—and wondered whether that was being strictly accurate. "And I promise not to rave. But I was disappointed and worried and I'm glad you had me over here to tell me."

A bell inside the entrance rang despotically and both of them jumped up. Laurie said, "Dick does admire you so, Jim. He can't stop talking about how you kept the team together in the pinches. Now I must run. Good night."

Jim got back into his car, divided in his mind between relief and dejection—relief, because Laurie's explanation was at least adequate; dejection, because Ted had won out, because he saw her daily, because of their years together. Friendship took time, and Jim knew enough about his feelings for girls to be certain that there must be friendship as a basis for any lasting ties.

He drove back home slowly, thinking over the brief talk. His habit of constancy, expectancy of good, and courage in distress helped him now. Thank goodness, he had Dick on his team! There was an ally. Laurie loved her brother, and Jim knew that anything he did for Dick was also a tie with her. Then came the thought of Dick's slowness in learning, and it was as if a cloud had come over the rising moon. If he substituted Rink Davis for Dick, what would Laurie say? What would she *feel?* If a man was 90 per cent feeling and 10 per cent mind-work, what about girls? They were *all* feeling. Well, there was one solution. He must coach Dick—or lay him off. And of course Laurie would appreciate his extra effort.

All in all, it had not been a bad evening, despite the shortness of time with Laurie and her confession about Ted.

15

On the Way

THE WEDNESDAY of the Burnsbrook-Hinsdale game arrived with clouds and enough humidity to wash a car in, but no wind. Jim's three carloads of athletes, plus Frank and Mr. McNail, entered the town through a factory district dense with smoke and decorated with used-car dumps and a frieze of tin cans.

"If they're as tough as this town looks, we've got a job on our hands!" Rod Kregill exclaimed.

"Tough is right," Goat Edwards agreed. "I hear they don't let anyone on the team until he's killed his man, or at least a boy."

"It's not that bad," Sam Slant said. "They don't allow kids to have firearms until they're six."

"That still leaves them knives and brass knuckles," Garry contributed. "Many a time I've seen bodies dangling from the trees—in the early morning, that is."

"It's hard to believe you," Jim said, "because you never lived here and, besides, you don't get up that early."

"Look!" Goat exclaimed. "There's Ike Morse's car. I reckon we'd better win, after all."

The owner-editor of *The Village News* greeted the Burnsbrook team by saying, "I came to see you extend your winning streak of one. You look sharp as my pencil. These boys are good, even if Ironwood School took them 3 to 2. Their unspoken object is to wipe you out, and I was happy to tell their coach that they couldn't do it."

A neatly uniformed cluster of players gathered from the field and Jim saw that their coach was spectacled and with a may-the-best-fellow-win sort of face, round, almost jolly, all of which belied the rumors of toughness. He shook hands with Frank Lafferty and said, "They shelled us over your way on Saturday, which means hard luck for you."

"I don't see the connection," Uncle Frank replied.

"Let me make it plain. Our plan is never to have two consecutive defeats."

"Do your plans always work out?" Goat asked of the player who was standing nearest.

"Well, mostly," the player answered, and a few of the Hinsdalers were seen to smile.

"Silence!" commanded the coach with mock severity. "When I make a qualified statement, I want no comment."

At this, several of his players chuckled, and their coach said to Frank, with exaggerated resignation, "Well, you see I have no control of them off the field. But when they're playing, watch out. When I suggest a home run, they oblige."

"For my part, I just let my boys go ahead and make their home runs, one after another," Frank said with an equally straight face.

"Well, we'll see which system works best," the Hinsdale professor said.

The Burnsbrookers listened with covert amazement. They

had been led to expect hard guys, bruisers, and, instead, they saw a youthful group of pleasant-faced athletes under the tutelage of a wise-cracking gentleman.

"It's confusing," Jim said as they walked over to their bench. "I bet they *are* hard, underneath, and just put on all this banter to fool us."

"Uncle Frank wasn't far behind them himself," Garry Steep commented with a wide grin.

Frank Lafferty and Jim had decided to run the same batting order that had been so successful in the Cedarlane game. Chuck Young walked to the plate and half the team envied his shoulders. Jim wondered whether a kid's envy of older boys helped his growth. He was satisfied to have that part of his life behind him. It took years from the time you wished you were a man until you became one, and those mid-teens were a rough cross-country the entire way.

All eyes were on the pitcher. His obvious back muscles could enable him to put strong stuff on the ball—if he had the follow-through. The thighs had the say, the basic power, given a proper pivot as he rolled into action. Frank had explained this to Tony years ago, and Tony had learned to save his arm by giving the work to his thighs and the pivot. The Hinsdale pitcher's delivery was enviably smooth.

Chuck readied himself for the first pitch and was still watching as it sizzled past him. The rather diminutive umpire called it a strike. The second pitch, a bit lower, a mite faster, was a strike.

"He looks rapid to me," Rod Kregill said.

The third pitch was a called strike, and when Chuck rejoined his fellows, Jim asked him what was the matter.

"He's never heard of a speed limit," Chuck said disgustedly. "Those balls were straight down the groove, and they got faster as they came. I'll get him the next time."

Kregill did a fair copy of Chuck's act, except that he

swung on the second and third pitches. "The guy's monotonous," he reported to the bench. "There's nothing on the ball I could see."

"That was the nothing you hit," Goat said, and the others laughed.

Jim walked out determined to solve this puzzle. A nothing-on straight ball ought to be easy to hit, however fast. The Hinsdale pitcher paused as if reading Jim's mind, changed the pace, and Jim connected, a shade too low, and the ensuing foul was caught by the third baseman.

"That's about as quick an inning as you'll see," Frank said. "Now let's put them in their places. Sharp does it."

"Toss them tricky," Jim said to Tony on the way out, and Tony complied. He threw a pronounced sinker first, a low curve considerably inside second, a fast corner-cutter third, and the Hinsdale batter threw his bat halfway to the bench.

To the next Hinsdaler, Tony reversed the order of his pitches and benched the batter in about ninety seconds. For the third, he started with the corner-snipper, followed with the sinker, and got the man out with a fast ball that broke in like a scared hare.

Jim felt somewhat easier. They had to outlast the others, that was all, and Tony could last. His hurt leg had stopped bothering him and he was ready for a pitcher's duel.

This is what the game became—a question of nerves. Everything else was right: the thin clouds eliminated sunglare, the slight breeze was cooling, the umpire was highly competent and leaned over backward to be fair. The rumors of toughness were a joke, a smoke screen for as good-natured opponents as Jim had ever played. The game would go to the team whose nerve held longest.

By the fifth inning, the strain began to tell. There had been a scattering of hits. Dick Anderson had reached first, and Roy Mason had slammed a two-bagger, but wilted on the vine. Jim had connected for a base hit, but was left there to die. Tony had held Hinsdale to three hits also. Then, at the top of the sixth, the change came. Tony was up, and his aim in life was to show that a pitcher could hit as well as anyone else, despite the legend. It was ridiculous, he insisted, to have the eyesight a pitcher must possess and not use it at bat.

So this time, while he waited, as always, for a pitch he liked, it finally came. The Hinsdale thrower had perhaps grown overconfident, for he unloosed a fat one at Tony, down the favorite groove, but no express pitch this time. Tony watched it ease along and clouted it high and far, right off the field for two bases. Then Chuck Young upped the ball and was caught. Rod Kregill slammed out a grounder that got through between first and second and brought Tony in. Jim hit into right field for a single, with Rod reaching third. Roy Mason was lucky, for he sliced two fouls without being caught. Then he drove a hot grounder through the pitcher, bringing Rod home, advancing Jim to second and reaching first himself.

"They're on the run," Frank said. "Keep them going."

Sam Slant obliged by connecting for the first time that afternoon. It was a near homer, bringing Jim in and Mason to third, while Sam slid, for a touchy near-tie with the ball, to second. The benevolent umpire called him safe. Jim hoped it was not harmful to be so satisfied with things: 3 to 0 and only one man down.

It was harmful, he soon decided. Frank had told Garry Steep to bunt, which he did, but not far enough. The catcher swooped out, slammed the ball to third, ousting Sam, and the third baseman threw to first in time to get Garry, a masterly rifle-shot that the crowd applauded.

"Let's better our lead," Frank urged as his men started to work. "Don't give them a base."

The Burnsbrookers obeyed, and presently they reached the top of the seventh inning, the last. The trouble with being visitors, Jim realized, was that the home team secured the second-thoughts end of the game. There was no way to get back at them if they tied or bettered your score. You had to get back at them first and run up a secure lead. What was a good lead against Hinsdale? He did not feel too secure with his 3 to 0.

Because of this lead, perhaps, Goat Edwards got no wood on the ball, and Dick Anderson followed Goat's example. Dick had done less than little all afternoon, Jim noted, and this failure precipitated the latter's emotional problem again. *Must* he put Rink Davis in Dick's place at right field? How much longer could he withhold Rink for his possible use as relief pitcher? That excuse was weak. Jim postponed decision now, at any rate, and forced his attention back to the field, in time to see Tony fly out to right field, directly into the fielder's mitt.

"Let's dig in, fellows," Jim said as they walked out.

"One play at a time, that's all," Frank repeated. It was his daily, hourly advice.

Ike Morse sat down beside Frank and said, "A good game—so far. I've got a column out of it. Jim deserves victories. I observed him more closely than he realized during that trip to Florida. I've never seen a cleaner lad with a steadier head."

"He's lucky in his home life," Frank replied. "That's half of any success."

"Fully half," Ike conceded. "But the other half is Jim's own doing. I like the way he persists."

"That's Jim," Uncle Frank concurred. "I wonder if all Scots are as stubborn. If Jim can't get over an obstacle, he goes around; if he can't go around, he burrows under; if he can't burrow under, he builds a ladder. I often wonder what his final ambition will be."

Ike's voice lowered. "Jean tells me that Jim is devoted to the Anderson girl."

"Jean's a competent observer," Frank said with a chuckle. "It hasn't hurt his game any. *Gosh!*"

A terrific crack of the bat was followed by a ball beyond the left fielder's reach. Frank's mouth stayed open as the Hinsdale batter reached second, raced to third, started home, and was waved back to third by the coach, just in time to welcome the ball.

"That's a sub," Frank said. "The guy at bat's another. I hope he's no twin."

Frank's hopes were dashed fast, for, in spite of a tricky curve, the Hinsdaler drove the ball over the shortstop, and it took a peculiarly sharp drop before the left fielder could get under it and complicated matters by a sidewise bounce. Result—one run for Hinsdale and one man on second.

Still another sub was sent in. Tony pitched a fast ball that sliced the corner at the same time that the batter was creaming it into the cloudy yonder above right field. Dick Anderson misjudged when to turn after running back and the batter reached third. The scoreboard read: Visitors 3, Hinsdale 2.

"I don't get this," Rink said. "Why'd their coach save up his stars? See, still another sub?"

Frank walked out to the mound where Jim was talking with Tony. "You're not tired," Frank said to the pitcher.

"No—only tired of being hit."

"Well, give him your death-warrant missile," Frank said.

Jim walked back to the plate. "All settled?" the batter asked with a confident smile.

"Too soon, fellow—better stow that smile," Jim warned him.

"I don't see why." The fellow's smile expanded. "It's all over, if you ask me."

"That suits me," said Jim, willfully mistaking the batter's meaning.

"Not the way I mean," the batter retorted.

"Play ball," the umpire cut in.

Tony's so-called death warrant was simply a fast, low, and inside ball, but faster, lower, and nearer inside than a batter need expect. It came. The batter returned it at turf-top level, just outside Tony's reach. The man at third scored the tying run, the batter reached first.

Jim signaled a repeat and Tony repeated. The batter struck out, and hope lifted its head again. True, the score was 3 to 3, with one Hinsdaler on first, but a tie gave Burnsbrook another chance to smother the foe.

Tony had stopped allowing hits. The second man struck out. Tony pitched. "Strike!" called the umpire. Tony pitched again. "Strike two!" Tony pitched, but with too little deceit rubbed into the cowhide.

Jim knew by the sound that it was above Anderson's head. The right fielder ran, raced, held out his hand, missed, ran on, threw to third, but the runner had cleared third. The throw was wild and, while Mason did his best, his throw to Jim was half a second late. The game was lost.

The Burnsbrookers' drive home was not jubilant. The other members of the team hated to lose, but did not realize what his loss had done to Jim's prospects. He had hoped to confront Ironwood School with three victories. Otherwise, the challenge by the Burnsbrookers could be shrugged off. Well, Cliffside remained. If they could beat Cliffside, who had beaten Ironwood, there was still a chance. But he had to bench Anderson, that was certain.

16

"Whoever Saw a Yes-Cat?"

FAMILY LIFE does not subsist on honey, not even Burnsbrook Farm honey, which Scott declared was "made by bees with happy thighs." The McNail family also flourished on a give-and-take of opinion.

Mr. McNail fondly declared that his wife had agreed with him just once—when she promised to marry him. Jim and Scott viewed nearly everything from opposite sides, except meals, which they were both in favor of, although they preferred different foods. Jean was a free lance, siding now with one and now with the other.

Even the Burnsbrook pets, Jim's Bogie and Jean's cat of many names, differed so deeply that they lived in a watchful truce. Jean stood up forcefully for her cat's rights in the household, while Jim contended for his dog's position. On no subject did he argue with his sister more continuously than on the inward nature of his dog.

On the Sunday morning after the Hinsdale game, the subject of canine supremacy had come up again at breakfast. Jim attributed Bogie's occasional yieldings to the cat's demands to his dog's natural chivalry and worldly wisdom. Jean said it was plain fear.

"What on earth would Bogie be afraid of?" Jim asked with some heat. "Certainly not of your William."

"Her name is no longer William the Conqueror but Eve, the wisest woman in the world."

"Would you mind telling me why Bogie should fear your William-Eve?"

"Simply watch them for one minute and you will see for yourself. Which person has the real assurance—a slave or the slave-master? The slave-master, naturally, and your dog is the almost perfect slave. You even *like* him for it, while I rejoice that Eve will never, *never* obey me unless she wants to."

"More silly reasoning!" Jim said as he poured honey on his hot cakes. "Do you call yourself a slave because you obey Mom and Pop?"

"No, because I like to do what they want me to."

"Oh, yes?" Jim said quickly. "I remember how gladly you didn't eat that third piece of chocolate cake last night when told not to. You pouted to show how glad you were. I remember how beautifully obedient you used to be about going to bed at eight o'clock. What nonsense you do bring up, Jean, just because you wish to win an argument!"

Jean tried from a new angle. "Bogie is a yes-dog, Jim. You have to admit that. Whistle and he drops everything and comes, even if the everything is a horrid rat. Push him away and he goes, as if he had no mind of his own, which is only too likely. He is so perfectly abject that Eve laughs at him."

"Oh, yes?" Jim said again, although he was secretly proud of Jean's countering his flawless arguments with plain nerve. "It's funny I never heard her laugh, or even smile."

"She's smiling now," Jean said and pointed to the gorgeous tortoise shell, who was indeed looking at Jim with a curious expression. "You don't hear her laugh, of course. She has more *tact* than many people I know. But to go back to Bogie, whoever heard of a yes-*cat?*"

Scott entered the room just then, and was struck by the somewhat belligerent attitude of the debaters. "Am I butting in on anything?" he asked, but sat down.

"Yes, thank goodness!" Jean said. "We need a referee." She, too, poured honey on her cakes. "I claim that Bogie does whatever Jim asks, no matter how silly, while my cat has a will, an independence that marks her superiority over any slave-dog."

"So cats must be the unhappiest animals on earth," Scott said blandly, by habit, because the brothers always teamed up against their sister. ("They like the sides to be even," Jean had once loftily declared.) "If you can't say *Yes* sometimes, you get mighty lonely." Then, dismissing Jean's heated reply, Scott told Jim that Frank wanted to see him. "He has been waiting for you to put Rink Davis in Dick Anderson's place at right field. He's feeling a little miffed by your delay and said to me, 'What's Jim playing for—the game or the girl?' "

"I guess Uncle Frank has eyes," Jean observed tartly. The brothers turned on her as one and Jim told her to go hunt mice so that Eve might respect her. Jean, who at heart wished to be in good graces with her brothers, collected a few dishes and carried them to the kitchen.

"Thanks for the tip," Jim said to Scott. "I'll go talk to him now."

Jim walked out into the May morning and wished he had an answer to Frank's question. He wanted both the girl and the game, meaning victory. Both were essential to his future. Some connection with Ironwood School seemed the clear road to his life ahead, and he was coming to feel the same way about Laurie. She was utterly different from the string of girls who had entered and exited from his life. Laurie lived in his thoughts, in his feelings, in his hopes. Never had he realized this so clearly as he did on his way to the barn where Frank would be scalding out the milk utensils.

The May morning was in love with the countryside, and Jim felt out of step with himself, out of tune with the soft air, the new turf, the apple blossoms in the orchard. For a long time now he had striven to make his ball team good enough to play the best—even Ironwood School. Was Ironwood first now? He had to be honest. Laurie was the all-important one, not just a passing excitement in his blood. This must be love, he thought, the kind of love which made you value a girl so much that you would do nothing to lessen her respect for you.

Then his thoughts took another turn that stopped him thinking of himself. What about *her* self-respect? She knew baseball. She must know that her brother, while playing good ball, was the least able player on the team. Why should she turn against him for pulling Dick out and putting Rink in? Maybe she wouldn't, but Jim had watched Jean too long and well to be sure. He remembered her warning that emotion decided everything—well, 90 per cent of everything, leaving 10 per cent to intellect. Laurie loved her gay and able brother, loved him quite possibly more than she loved herself—and certainly her self-respect. Dick himself was a great guy. He would say nothing in protest, however he might feel the ouster.

Frank had finished the indoor chores and was gazing at the distant orchard. "I reckon another spraying's due. Why does nature put up with pests?" he asked.

"She plays fair," Jim answered.

"By gummy, you may be right. I never thought of that."

Jim came straight to the point. "Scott tells me you think it's time to put Rink in Dick Anderson's place."

Uncle Frank shot an inquiring look at the boy. "Nobody likes Dick better than I do, Jim, or I'd've insisted on the change weeks ago. But even the fellows are hinting about it now. Rink has grown while we stand and look. It was touch and go with Cedarlane and Hinsdale, but Cliffside's a different matter. They beat Ironwood, don't forget."

Jim reached his decision. He said, "I'll tell Dick today."

"I can tell him," Frank offered. "After all, I'm the coach."

"I'm still manager," Jim countered. "Besides—"

"I know," Frank said. "Drat the girl! There's always a girl in every jam, seems to me. Without her being his sister, there'd be nothing to it, except a matter of throwing and hitting."

"She knows baseball," Jim began.

"As if that mattered!" Frank exclaimed. Jim almost smiled at their complete agreement on feminine reasoning. "You could begin with her, though, sort of ask her advice."

Jim shook his head. "They don't like us to hide behind their skirts, Frank."

"You're right. How do you know so much about women, boy? You don't get around like Scott."

"I've lived with two all my life," Jim reminded him. "A guy ought to get onto something in that time." Then he started toward the orchard. At least it offered no problems for the moment.

After midday dinner, Jim strolled down to the lane's end, for he wanted to flag Dick and straighten things out alone. But when the car appeared, Jim saw, to his discomfiture, that Laurie was sitting beside her brother. "She's taking a weekend," Dick explained. "I thought I'd bring her along as sub-coach."

Jim bade her welcome in any capacity, while his mind was turning over like a racer's engine, and trying to beat down his heart. How could he open the subject now? Yet why not? It might even be better this way. Before he could arrange his thoughts, his words started to pour out from deep within him. "It's fortunate I can see you both like this."

Laurie instantly sensed that something was amiss and asked, "Why, Jim, what's wrong?"

"Something that's been hard to get off my chest, Laurie."

"Get in." Dick leaned across his sister's knees to open the door. "For Pete's sake, what's the matter?"

"It's about you," Jim said, without getting in the car. "Frank says—that is, both Frank and I think that Rink Davis has come along so fast, especially as a batter, that he ought to start—against Cliffside."

Laurie got it at once and demanded sharply, "Instead of Dick?"

"That's the size of it," Jim answered, hurting at her tone.

"I don't think much of that!" Laurie retorted with heat.

"Now, Sis! You're not running the team!" Dick broke in. "And it needn't be for keeps."

"It needn't be at all!" Laurie exclaimed. "Just because Dick had an off day—everybody does."

"Frank has watched Rink pull ahead in hitting and throwing, Laurie, and he thinks—"

"What do *you* think?" Laurie interrupted, and her eyes were blue ice. Jim was reminded for an instant of Jean in the kitchen, defending her cat.

"I think the same," Jim told her firmly. "Frank is impartial, Laurie. I can't be—and you know why."

It was a bold reply but Jim met Laurie's gaze straight on,

and, suddenly, her tone softened. "Are you manager or is Frank?" she asked in a different manner.

"Frank has coached Tony and me since we were kids, Laurie. He has almost never given us a bum steer. I am glad to rely on his opinion."

Dick had said nothing during this interchange. Now he spoke up. "Look, Sis, this is a game we're playing. Frank and Jim are right, and I think you know enough ball to realize it, too. Rink has come up and can hit better. It isn't a matter of opinion or prejudice. He just can. The plays are in the book. The point now is to beat Cliffside. Surely you agree about that."

There was the briefest pause, during which Jim lived an age. . . . Finally, Laurie said, "Yes, I spoke out of turn, so forget it." Then she moved closer to her brother and turned to Jim, "Get in–manager."

She had become the old Laurie again and Jim quickly crowded in beside her. These were his friends, whatever happened. Suddenly he felt load-free, lighter and happier than he had for a long, long time.

17

Cliff-hanging at Cliffside

FRANK LAFFERTY was ending his pep talk as the Burnsbrookers finished dressing in the locker room at Cliffside School. Jim usually set a good example by listening, but the craziest comedian on TV wouldn't have diverted his brooding at this juncture. This game settled his hash, fate, life, as his exaggerated emotion had it. If the team lost to Cliffside, after the Hinsdale defeat, there was small use trying to arrange a game with Ironwood School. He and his crowd wouldn't be even noticeable. But if Burnsbrook could beat, or even tie, champion Cliffside, Ironwood would have to notice.

It was almost a year since he had stood beside Laurie Anderson, watching Cliffside knock out Ironwood—a year since admission to his dream school had been denied him. A year was a long time to wait for something that had become as necessary to his happiness as his blood stream.

"All right, fellows, let's go," Frank said. "Play each minute as if it was the most important minute in your life. Don't think of what's gone or what's to come. Play *it*. Jim and I have changed the batting order to make use of Rink's long ball: Young–Kregill–McNail–Mason–Davis–Slant–Steep–Edwards–Wayland. We've got the day. You're rested. Let's bag this game."

Ike Morse had come to report the game personally for his *Village News*. At the end of the fourth inning, he laid down the yellow sheets of paper clamped to a board on the bench beside him and said to Frank, "If this keeps up, I can put it all in a headline–*No Hits, No Runs, No Interest*."

"Can't you admire good pitching when you see it?" Frank asked.

"I can also admire good hitting–*when* I see it."

"You're worse than the boys!" Frank objected. "I wear out my tongue telling them to be patient at the plate, to be watchful, to be on their toes–above all, to be patient. You'll see something soon. Something's got to break and it won't be Tony."

Three innings had ended in a stalemate, and the fourth added goose eggs to the score sheet. Ike burst out again, "I ask you *when* is the action to start? This bench is getting hard."

Jim's inner tension had been mounting, too. He, as well as Frank, knew that this strain of perfection, this utter balance of skill between pitchers and batters, could hardly go on much longer. After all, this was no World Series between champions. It was certainly wearing on the nerves. Each player's mind bore the burden of responsibility not to be the first to crack, and burdens have to be set down when they get too heavy.

The day was curiously perfect, windless, cloudless, just warm enough.

The Burnsbrookers walked back to their bench at the end of the fourth without talking. The spell could only be broken by the sound of wood on ball. Even the considerable crowd was unusually quiet, although growing restive. Like Ike Morse, they wanted action, not simply the compressed action of strike-outs but the roaring action of long hits, risky steals, double plays. And there were only three innings left!

"What do you say I start something?" Rod Kregill asked as he headed for the plate.

"That fellow's full of ideas," Goat said. Nobody laughed.

The Cliffside pitcher left fly—and so did Rod. The crack, pistol-sharp, brought the Burnsbrookers to their feet. The ball sailed safely over the center fielder's head, and Rod reached second safely.

Jim felt a load lifted as he went to bat. "To the right, hit to the right," he kept thinking. The first ball looked wide and he let it go. The umpire thought differently. The second looked low, and Jim passed it, too. The umpire rolled out, "Str-r-rike two!" Suddenly, Jim felt released and he stepped into the next one, clearly a curve, lining it out just inside the third base chalk. Rod slid past the third base bag but recovered in the nick of time.

Roy Mason stood at the plate. He was just naturally loose, a broad-shouldered statue of confidence. Cliffside's pitcher waved his outfield farther out, then hurled a hot ball above Roy's hip. The Negro stepped back, caught the ball on the top and drove it deep into right field. Rod came home. Jim tried for home and was thrown out. But they had one run at last and a good man on second!

Some very critical inspection was focused on Rink Davis by Dick Anderson. The substitute had yet to prove that he was so conspicuously better than Dick that his benching of the latter paid off. Frank, too, missed no motion of his bat or glove. The coach had taught Rink, when at bat, to prevent even a moment's inertia by constantly waving his stick. Frank had also got him to roll his wrists fast and so avoid a late swing. Rink was Frank's boy because he seemed never to forget what the man tried to teach him. He was one of those patient pupils, and his instructor hoped earnestly that this time up would show something.

Rink lost the first pitch for a called strike. He lost the second, an ornery sinker. Readying himself for the third, he watched and then drove, with every muscle of thigh, hip, waist, back, and arms descending on the ball. It leaped, flew, soared, riding ten feet over the stampeding center fielder's head to lose itself in the beyond. Rink's home run brought Mason in and the score was now a jubilant 3 to 0 for the invaders.

It is hard to stop a bonfire, once lighted, and the Burnsbrookers now flamed and crackled with unloosed energy. Sam Slant continued the rally with a two-base grounder, just inside the third base line. Garry Steep bunted—the first successful bunt of the afternoon. It was so well placed that the Cliffside catcher lost his eagerness to grab the ball and get it to first. He finally threw it a little aside from the baseman's reach and the umpire proclaimed Garry safe. Sam stopped at third.

Goat Edwards, as usual, had a wisecrack when he got up to bat. "See that red glow? It comes from the sunset of this pitcher's day."

Ike Morse laughed loudest of any at the remark. He said to Frank, "Even if that clown never hit, he'd pay for his ride."

"He can hit, too," Frank told him confidently.

The rally carried on through that inning, with two more runs, thanks to Goat's bringing in Sam, and Tony sending Goat home.

Cliffside rallied, too, but was deadlocked by a rash of

caught fouls. The score was still 5 to 0 for the Burnsbrookers after their last appearance at bat in the seventh.

"Now we've got to be on our toes for sure," Jim said as his team took the field. "Forget the score and play as if we had to knock down each man or lose the game." How he wished that his team had the last say at bat! That 5 to 0 looked huge, but letdowns were easiest then, for a big lead had a lulling effect.

Tony, fortunately, knew all about that temptation and wasted nothing. He was almost professionally steady in a pinch. Frank noticed that he had finally mastered the art of covering the ball before every pitch. No batter caught a wink of it. Only when the ball disappeared into his mitt and his arm lifted did he vary the grip on it to suit the pitch he intended to throw. Also, the large full circle his arm made had a relaxed suggestion that most batters misread. Now, instead of being overeager, Tony let go some of the finest pitches Jim had ever had the pleasure of stopping. Cliffside went down in a brilliant display of no-hitting, one, two, three.

As Jim walked over to Tony, to congratulate him, he had to control his voice, for he was deeply stirred. His wildest hope had become fact. It seemed incredible that the Burnsbrookers had paralyzed the winner over Ironwood by this clean-cut victory. Surely, *surely* Ironwood must recognize his team now and take up the challenge he would write out and deliver that evening.

The ride home was marred only by the team's being separated in four cars. Jim wished they could jubilate together. However, his mother had invited them all to another stand-up supper, and Burnsbrook Farm contained more concentrated joy that evening than it had ever seen before.

"How do you account for so one-sided a win?" Mr. McNail asked Frank Lafferty.

"I account for it because each player happened to do his best at the same time. That steam-rollered a mighty good team."

"Well, what did Cliffside do wrong?" Mr. McNail persisted.

"They couldn't hit Tony. That was it. And we did hit their pitchers. They didn't make many errors. Their umpire did the best he could for them, but he couldn't do much."

When the last crumb of cake and the last spoonful of ice cream had been disposed of, Jim said to a suddenly attentive audience, "Now about our game with Ironwood School. I'll ask for an exhibition game in midweek. Is there any Wednesday or Thursday that any of you can't get off?"

Frank brought out a calendar and said, "Let's offer dates. That pins it down tighter."

"Write it out now," Dick suggested. "I'll take it to Laurie. She'll want to hear the details of our game."

Jim looked at the clock. "You could phone her now instead. Until eight o'clock is the rule."

"As Jim happens to know," Tony said, and they all laughed.

"Maybe she could give you the name of the guy to phone to," Roy said.

"I don't think that's wise," Frank told him. "You just can't throw this at their coach. He might say *No* right off."

The team agreed with Uncle Frank, and Jim took Dick to the telephone. Dick dialed and, while they were waiting for Laurie, Jim said, "We're all mighty obliged to you, Dick." He knew that Laurie's brother would understand without his spelling it out.

"Rink's homer washed out any argument," Dick replied. Then Laurie was on the telephone and Dick said, "Get ready to take a blow, Sis. We creamed Cliffside 5 to 0."

Jim heard Laurie's "Oh! How *wonderful!*"

Dick gave her a quick run-down of the game, then said, "Jim's eavesdropping on all this. I can't drive him away."

"Idiot!" Laurie cried happily. "Let me–"

"You're talking to me now," Jim said.

"Oh, Jim, Jim, I'm so happy! You've stuck to your belief the whole time, too. I'm so proud of you all!"

"Now we want you to help us take Ironwood down a peg."

"How dreadful!" But Laurie laughed. "Now I've got to cheer for my school and kind of hope you'll win at the same time."

"We haven't got a game scheduled yet. That's where you come in, Laurie. Do you know anyone on the school staff who'd really like to accept our challenge?"

"Ted Everson would. I've been talking the Burnsbrookers up till he's madly jealous."

Dick took over the receiver and said, "Jim's been turned down every time he's asked for a game, Sis. Can you–"

"Don't hustle me!" Laurie urged excitedly. "This has got to be schemed out. Ted will know. Let me speak to him–and I can't do it now. I've got to be in study hall. But tomorrow–tomorrow I'll have word for you sure."

18

The Game

THE DAYS following Jim's challenge to Ironwood School were hard on the McNail household. Jim's mother grieved silently because of her sympathy with her son's state of mind. His father was glad of his son's perseverance and the way that his eldest was showing self-control. Scott, with unusual tact, held his tongue. But Jean could not stand the suspense and burst out with, "I don't see it. All they've got to do is say *Yes* or *No*. It oughtn't to take six days to do that."

On the seventh day, Laurie telephoned. "Ted can't get a decision from Coach Appleton, Jim. If he says *No*, I'm going straight to Mr. Ironwood and tell him how long you've worked to get your team ready to *beat* Ironwood, and it's up to Ironwood to prove that it can't be taken. Mr. Ironwood's a great man. He understands greatness and he can recognize it in others. I think you're great, Jim. The way you stick at a thing shows it."

Since Jim never knew how to meet an extravagant compliment and usually tried to laugh it off, he replied, "Mom thinks so, too, Laurie. But she thinks Scott is great, too. And Pop. And Jean. And she's got a high opinion of your brother, too."

"I'm not sure I like crowds," Laurie came back with a giggle. "But I'll go for this one. Keep on being great."

Two hours later, Coach Appleton telephoned. When he was assured that he was talking with the manager of the Burnsbrookers, he said, "We accept your offer of a practice game, if you can play this coming Wednesday, the thirteenth."

"We can. What time?"

"Two o'clock. The visitors' clubhouse is yours after one."

"We'll be there, cloud or shine."

"It had better shine. We have no other open dates."

Before he slept that night, Jim had reached every team member and all agreed to be at Ironwood promptly by one-fifteen of the thirteenth.

Jim slept well that night, although it took a while to drowse off. His long-held ambition was coming true at last, and Laurie had helped. Laurie, in some way or other, was always helping. Well, he'd help her someday. That kept him awake a while longer. His thoughts at times had become the same as a man's, Jim told himself. Maybe he was a man then, even though he slid back. Maybe you grew up by taking three steps forward and only two back, the way spring came toward summer. Laurie and spring were much alike, and they did the same things to your spirits.

Wednesday's sky was clouded, but the clouds burned away by noon. Mrs. McNail had an early lunch ready for the game-goers of her family, but she would not go along to Ironwood with them.

"You have to, Mom," Jim urged. "I want you there."

"You forget I'm having twelve guests for supper, Son."

"We'll be too happy to eat, Mom, as the song says."

"That song writer didn't know much about boys."

They all begged in turn but the homemaker would not be persuaded.

For Jim the morning had dragged and he had wished he was living in tomorrow—by then, the game would be ancient history. Yes, but what kind of history? What if they lost to Ted Everson's pitching? Over and over, Jim had switched his mind away from the edge of that precipice!

Jim left the farm with Frank Lafferty, before the McNail trio of rooters, in order to be at the clubhouse well ahead of the others. Some of the pressure lifted as the team began to arrive. The fellows looked hearty and not visibly nervous. But for them this was just a game, a special game, but still a game, while for him it was a symbol of his future, his entrance exam into another world, his way of announcing to the Ironwood world that he was somebody and worth paying attention to in the future.

The boys were impressed by the visitors' quarters below the gymnasium. They dressed quietly, for game time was nearing.

"What's keeping Rink?" Tony asked Belt Burrows. "Weren't you to bring him?"

"He phoned that his family was bringing him."

One-thirty arrived, but no Rink. Jim said, "Frank, you'd better take them out for the warm-up. I'll phone Rink."

Jim pushed away the black gloom that had been descending on his spirits. Now that he might be deprived of Rink's arm, he realized how much more dependable he was than Dick Anderson. No one answered the Davis telephone.

This meant that they must be on their way, lost perhaps, held up by the traffic, but coming.

Rink did not come, but the onlookers did. Ironwood's students filled one stand and at least as many spectators arrived from Ironwood Village, where Ike Morse had plugged for the game in his paper.

Sam Slant, watching Ted Everson take his throws, said, "He sure whips that ball across like the lash of a mule whip."

"Yes, but he learned it off a frog," Goat Edwards declared. "It jumps like one, and his curve could double for a rainbow."

"He must have some weak spot," Garry Steep said hopefully.

"Push and rush," Frank said. "He'll wear out in five innings at his gait, let alone seven."

Two o'clock arrived but no Rink, and Frank announced, "We'll play our old batting order. The ump's gone out. Chuck, you're up. Just play one play at a time."

Chuck Young made a sturdy figure out there in the sunlight. He looked at the first pitch—high. Everson lowered the next pitch and Chuck fouled, but safely. The next two pitches were balls and Rod Kregill said, "Everson's not sudden death, anyway."

"Three and one," Garry said. "Chuck'll wait."

"Chuck likes rules, they're so easily broken," Goat said. "What'd I tell you!" he exclaimed as Chuck reached for the next and knocked a half-hearted ball to the pitcher. Everson slammed it to first base, yards ahead of the batter.

When the flushed Chuck arrived at the bench, Jim said, "How's Ted look close up?"

"He's no flame-thrower. I shouldn't have reached for that ball."

"It's cagey pitching to tease a batter into reaching," Frank told him.

"Who said he teased me?" Chuck asked angrily. He caught fire easily.

"Most batters watch the first two pitches," Jim said, to ward off gunfire. "So the cagey pitcher tricks them into a hole that way. Then they've got to hit the one he's been saving. You broke up his plans, Chuck."

Newspaperman Morse, sitting with the boys, looked his praise of Jim's tactful peacemaking. He said to Tony quietly, "Jim ought to work for the State Department as trouble-shooting diplomat."

Tony was hardly listening. He was watching Kregill, who had lingered into the same hole: two called strikes.

"Some days, Rod leaves his long hits in the car," Sam Slant observed.

Rod swung at the Everson fast one too late and returned to the bench. Jim walked out with the weight of a freight car on his shoulders. Then Goat shouted something that Jim didn't catch. "What'd he say?" he asked the Ironwood catcher.

"Some joke about the Scotchman being tight."

"Not me," Jim said and he felt the looseness coming. He had stood at the plate behind the barn hundreds of times, as loose as a scarecrow. He pictured the scarecrow flapping in the breeze. His shoulders eased. Ted threw. Jim got a head start on the ball which rose and flew. Jim pounded toward first, but a roar from the Ironwood stand told him the news—the left fielder had gloved it.

Three down in a row! Loping back for his glove, Jim reached Tony and Frank. The coach was saying to his pitcher, "Count ten—and you've got them."

Tony nodded. He would. He would do everything he had ever been told, once he rid himself of this armor that encased him so rigidly. He had never been this tight. But then he had never pitched in a game so important as this. He reached the rubber and sent the first of his free throws to Jim. It landed precisely where Jim had pointed. He threw again—right. And again—right.

Frank Lafferty felt a slow fire in his middle. He cared about this game more than any game since his days as a pro. The boys had worked for it, and they were lucky in being able to forget themselves in the play. A coach had to sit it out.

Tony threw his best brand of fast ball—a called strike. Then a ball that looked as if it had bitten off the far corner of the plate—another strike.

"He's set," Frank said to Ike Morse.

"It's not only the ball he covers," Morse said. "Look at his face. Talk about wooden Indians. Except he's kind of white."

"*Ster-rike!*" called the umpire.

The second Ironwooder faced Tony and the umpire repeated his "*Ster-rike!*"

"The batter's still figuring how it got past him," Frank said.

Belt Burrows edged a little nearer to Frank and said, "You got to hand it to Tony. Nothing ever jolts him. You might suppose he was working behind the barn."

The second batter retired and a long, limber Ironwood boy did a slow dance with his bat. "He's supposed to be confusing the pitcher," Frank interpreted, "Tony'll confuse him with a row of change-ups."

This Tony did—a slider, a horseshoe curve, a fast one with a deceitful kink in it.

As the fielders returned to the bench, a panting boy came running up and asked, "Is Jim McNail here?"

Jim beckoned and the boy said, "A phone call from your Rink Davis. He says to tell you that he was run into by a truck. Nobody hurt, but the front wheel's out of line. He's going to try to get a hitch here. He's at Northrow."

That was ten miles away. The game would be half done. But still— A shout went up. Roy Mason had plugged a hot one to the outfield. But the center fielder was under it. "Well, he can be hit, anyway," Frank said to the returning Roy. "Thanks for showing us."

But Sam Slant could not connect in his three tries. "What were you doing? Waving to some girl in the stands?" Goat questioned.

"I don't think that guy threw a ball," Sam answered. "If he did, I didn't see it."

"Fast hands, Garry, fast hands," Frank explained as Steep headed for the plate. "Don't try too hard."

Garry endeavored not to try too hard and he had a cure that worked. He imagined himself back on the lot behind the Ironwood Village movie house, where he had played as a kid and it was all fun. You hit or you didn't hit and the talk was for fun, too. Now he gripped his bat, planted his spikes in the spring turf, struck so hard that he did a circle himself, but the catcher returned the ball to Everson and said to Garry, "If you feel dizzy, just lean on me."

"Thanks, smart guy." Garry hit the next ball high, wide, and far, but it came down like its predecessor—in the center fielder's glove.

"Good boy," Frank said to Garry. "Next time you'll find the spot."

Burnsbrook retired and Tony took to the mound. He downed the first and second Ironwood batters in seven throws. Laurie Anderson sat taut, her hands clenched. This was no game for her. Too much mattered, and all the worse because she must not betray her feelings. She was sitting next to Paul Atwood, dean of admissions, who asked her, "Who is that one-man firing squad?"

"Tony Wayland, a farmer's son living next to Jim McNail. You remember Jim."

"It comes back to me, regretfully. The boy who wanted to be a day student and play ball for us. I wish we could have nabbed him."

"He's *made* his team," Laurie said tensely.

"Is he headed for the pros?"

A crack of the bat stopped Laurie's explanation of Jim's future, as he had confided it to her. Ted Everson had caught Tony's curve at the precise moment of maximum momentum. The ball fell slightly beyond Dick Anderson, but he recovered in time to reach Mason at third as Ted was sliding in, and the umpire signaled *out*.

"Nifty fielding," Dean Atwood commented.

"It's my brother playing right field," Laurie said.

"Two of a kind, eh?" Atwood smiled at the flushed girl.

"No, I throw left-handed," Laurie said deftly.

"You know how to field compliments. I can see you've had long practice."

Laurie fielded that one by explaining that Jim had taken his team all the way to Florida to train. "This game means an awful lot to him."

Mrs. Atwood leaned across her husband to say to Laurie, "A little bird tells me that he means a lot to you."

"What nonsense!" Paul Atwood exclaimed. "Can't you see she's wearing a school pin, honey?"

"Justice means a lot to me," said Laurie without smiling.

The game permitted small time for verbal conflict, however. Back at the bench, Jim was saying, "This time up has got to do it. We have Everson's range. Now let's knock him off the rubber."

The Goat was up, short but strong and wiry, and he hit Everson's first pitch over the center fielder's head. Only exceptionally able throwing saved a home run. The Village contingent shouted appreciation–and hope.

Frank Lafferty slapped Dick Anderson on the shoulder. "Now bring him in. Just watch the ball and hit what you see."

But "just" watching the Everson ball was a big order. Ted threw low and fast, with a snaky curve to boot, and Dick did not connect. With two strikes against him, he did catch a piece of the ball and achieved an easily caught foul.

Tony Wayland walked to the plate with Jim's voice in his ear, "Slam it to your favorite spot, boy." Tony did intend to shoot a grounder inside first and right field, but the ball rose one floor too high and the right fielder made his third put-out of the game.

"We can't leave Goat there," Frank said to Chuck Young. "Just one nice clean little hit into the great open spaces."

Chuck drilled a nice clean little hit into the great open glove of the center fielder–and that was that.

Jim swallowed his bitter disappointment and said, "We can do better than this–and will."

Tony faced the end of Ironwood's batting order with confidence. The numbness of his first minutes was gone. Even when the first man up hit a two-bagger by mastering Tony's sinker, Tony fended off alarm. The next man would naturally bunt or sacrifice in some other way, and Tony aimed to foil that. You can't bunt a ball you don't see; so Tony flung one–chin-high, a ball, but no bunt. He sent the next across the letters for a called strike. Jim signaled for the same above the knee, and Tony obliged. Strike two.

Jim now asked for a sinker, but Tony shook that off. He was in firm control. Why not wipe out the batter with one more express-speed ball across the guy's middle? Jim, strangely, insisted, and Tony obeyed. But the sinker sank too soon, hit the plate and bounced away past Jim's reach. The Ironwooder made third.

"My fault," Tony said as Jim reached him.

"Forget it," Jim told him. "Choose your throw."

Tony decided on another fast one at midriff. It all but singed the youth at bat, who said, "Control yourself out there. My head's not insured."

"Why should it be?" cracked Tony, but he was troubled. Jim might be right, so Tony threw a second sinker. The Ironwood coach was probably demanding a squeeze play, and the best way to break that up was to drill his pitches past the batter. A batter determined to bunt was nearly impossible to stop. But Tony had often put the impossible in its place. So now he returned to his fast one, but his toe slipped, and the batter did bunt. But not successfully, for the ball did not roll far enough to elude the charging Jim, who slammed it to first in time to tag the runner three feet off the plate.

"Remind me to breathe," Paul Atwood said to his wife.

"I stopped that long ago," she replied.

Laurie realized that her fingernails were digging into her palms and relaxed a little, but that subconscious action of her hands answered the question as to where her heart lay. She was glad, *glad* that Jim had beat the runner out. Glad? She ought to be ashamed of herself, secretly rooting for the Burnsbrookers. But wasn't her brother a Burnsbrooker? Nonsense, her conscience told her. Be honest with yourself, please. You haven't given a thought to your brother. It's Jim you're glad for, and let Ted Everson find it out, if he can. Then the eternal womanly need to hide her feelings took over. And when Dean Atwood said to her, "Nice play, even if it did us out of a run," Laurie could reply, "Ironwood will wake up soon."

So far nothing but goose eggs decorated the scoreboard. The Ironwood players may have consoled themselves by pretending that they were just idling along, with nothing to worry about, and they would get going soon. But the game was half over, and when Rod Kregill came to bat, Ironwood had a scare. He met the Everson meteor on the nose and drove it out of the field for a home run.

It was at this moment that Headmaster Ironwood IV arrived at the stand and sat down between his Dean of Admissions and Laurie. "Who's that rascal who dares make a home run at our expense?" he exclaimed.

Laurie enlightened him and added, "This boy at bat is Jim McNail, organizer and captain of the Burnsbrook team."

"And if you want to know anything more about Jim, ask Laurie here. I believe she is doing a term paper on him," Paul Atwood said with a straight face.

"Master Paul passed his course in kidding," Laurie said to Mr. Ironwood. "Jim McNail has lived years for that run. He wanted more than anything to play ball for Ironwood, but the school regulations ruled him out. So he got up this team to show—to show he could—"

Her voice choked and Laurie turned her face away, for sudden unexplained wetness scalded the lids of her eyes. She always felt this way when she read beautiful poetry or saw somebody being great and courageous or when her team won. Everybody else seemed able to laugh and beat each other on the back, but she wanted to cry—for joy. She must be simple-minded. She barely caught the end of Mr. Ironwood's sentence ". . . I'm glad such persistence succeeds, but he mustn't carry it too far. I can't have Ironwood beaten just to suit that boy's ambition, no matter how much he deserves it. Now who is up?"

"Roy Mason, the third baseman," Laurie said. "I met him. He has the nicest manners."

"Then maybe he won't be rude to us and knock another homer," Mr. Ironwood said.

"He's good," Dean Atwood told him. "He got Jameson out on a throw to first that any professional would have been proud of."

Mason proceeded to back up Atwood's praise by whaling a grounder through Everson by a mitt-length and making first.

"Come, come!" Mr. Ironwood exclaimed. "Doesn't Ted know that you're watching?" he asked Laurie playfully.

To the girl, however, her divided loyalties were like a two-edged knife without a handle.

"And now your brother!" Mr. Ironwood noted as Dick Anderson strode to the plate. "This will never do! He—"

The Headmaster's words were lost in an uproar from the Village cheering section, for Dick smashed out a low comet-like hit between second and third, just above the shortstop's reach. Mason reached third safely, but Dick dared not risk trying for second, and wisely, for the Ironwood left fielder recovered skillfully and threw to second before Dick could have slid in.

"How's this batter?" Mr. Ironwood asked.

"He has done nothing so far. His name is Sam Slant."

"Slant?" Mr. Ironwood repeated. "We had to put his father's store out of bounds for our young men."

The sunny air was carrying plenty of noise by now. The Ironwood rooters were encouraging Ted Everson and discouraging the batters by turns. The umpire resorted to gestures. Sam let the first delivery go by, a ball; and the second, a called strike. Then he dented the horizon with a magnificent swing-and-hit. Mason loped home. Dick Anderson trotted home. Sam raced to third. The scoreboard read: *Visitors* 3, *Ironwood* 0.

"I feel like King Canute," Mr. Ironwood said. "But surely the tide must turn soon."

Garry Steep unfortunately fouled and was caught. Goat swatted into the pitcher's hands, and the side was out.

Tony walked to the mound thoughtfully. At last he had a margin but must waste nothing.

Ted Everson was up and he said to Jim, "We can take a joke, but 3 to 0 is too much humor for one afternoon."

"All right, we'll get serious," Jim replied, and signaled for Monday. Tony had a routine for each day of the week. Monday meant a fast-and-low pitch, a sinker, a U curve. But Ted got serious, too, and caught the curve for a two-bagger.

Ironwood's first baseman was up. Tony drilled in his fastest, close to the batter's chest. But his gangling contestant could read minds and stepped back just enough for the right purchase to drive the ball past Tony's shoulder. Ted Everson scored Ironwood's first run. The stands rose and roared. The batter slid safe to second and Ironwood continued to roar. Headmaster Ironwood applauded. Laurie clapped once. She felt heartsick, wishing this had not happened and fearful of the next play. Her whole being was in conflict with years of loyalty to her school. She dared not think of Ted.

The next Ironwood batter popped up a foul that Jim easily caught, and he felt better. But his relief was short-lived. The next batter bunted Tony's curve, and in the scramble for it, the Ironwooder on second made third. One run, one man on third, one down.

Frank Lafferty's face was drawn and Ike Morse said, "Jim will pull out of this."

"He has done it before," Frank said.

"So I've noticed," Ike agreed. "He always comes up for more, the way a man should."

"He's luckier than that. If he comes a cropper, he lands on a four-leaf clover."

"I hope he does it soon," Ike said. "This game has added ten years to my life."

It was at this minute that Rink Davis appeared, breathless and sorry. At the same time, a terrific crack of bat on ball indicated disaster. The ball soared out of sight—a home run, and Rink read the scoreboard with dismay: *Visitors* 3, *Ironwood* 3.

Tony waited for the noise to die down and then pitched the side out with magnificent control. As he walked in with Jim, he said, "I'm sorry. What did I do wrong?"

"Every pitch was good," Jim said. "They simply got to the ball. Now we've got to do the same. Look, here's Rink!"

Jim hated to demote Dick Anderson, who had been playing well, but Dick was, after all, a sub now, and Rink's lateness had not been his fault, so the substitution had to be.

Tony opened up the fifth inning with a fly over the shortstop's head, but the left fielder made a spectacular leap and speared it. Chuck Young whacked out a fierce grounder between first and second, the center fielder's ball. To the Burnsbrook bench it looked as if Chuck had tagged the bag a split second before the ball slapped into the baseman's mitt, but the umpire thought otherwise. Shouts of disapproval came from the Village stand.

Garry said to Sam Slant, "I bet that umpire was a successful chicken thief."

Chuck slogged back to the bench and spoofed to Rod

Kregill as he passed, "If your bat slips and bends the umpire's neck, I'll forgive you."

Laurie clasped her hands as she might have done in church during a prayer. "Anyway, it's not treason to wish your brother's side well," she said to herself, and the prayer must have had merit, for Kregill slapped the ball past the pitcher and made first.

Rink declared, "We're going places now," for Jim was up. And he did go—as far as first base on a clean grounder to the shortstop, whose throw, while able, was tardy. Mason drove Kregill and Jim each a base farther. Rink Davis walked to the plate, to Laurie's surprise. He knocked his first pitch skyward and was caught and the side was out.

Laurie was taut once more. Who said a ball game was fun? She had not suffered so much anxiety in her entire life.

Tony realized that a trial of his arm was coming. He had faced crises before and knew what to do—to slump in your skin and let yourself go loose to the fingernails. Only his eye must not slump. His eye was king, and the ball had to obey its command. Nature had fixed it that way. The eye was his mind, his arm, the ball's boss. See right, pitch right.

And so it went. The Village onlookers saw their young farm hand standing there, covering the ball, rearing back, firing. They saw the Ironwooders hitting—at ghosts. Not once did they connect. There were nine strikes in nine pitches, thrilling the stands, thrilling Laurie.

Even Mr. Ironwood was moved. "Extraordinary!" he exclaimed. "Most extraordinary! What's got into the boy?"

"His past," Laurie answered with understanding. "The McNail farm hand has been coaching pitcher and catcher ever since they were small boys."

Sam Slant opened the next to last inning with the score still tied at 3 each. "We've got to get a lead," Jim said.

Sam wanted to oblige. He wanted too hard and struck out. Garry Steep pulled a hit too far to the right and the first baseman nailed it. Goat warmed up on fouls and was caught on the third.

Tony had barely got his breath when he was on the mound again. Ironwood's second baseman was up; low and inside had worked before—and did this time. Tony threw a corner-clipper which the umpire called a ball. Tony warmed under the collar and translated that warmth into speed. The smoke from a fast one got into the batter's vision. He fouled and Jim raced back, back, holding out his mitt. The ball fell into it, bounced, was held. One down.

Tony remembered the next guy's liking the ball straight, no matter how fast, so pitched fantastic curves. Three times the batter struck in vain, then banged his bat away as if it had been at fault; two down.

The third Ironwooder hit, but Goat speared it, and Tony breathed again. He was still alive and one more inning to go. The cream of their list came up next time. Well, let it.

Burnsbrook opened the last inning with Tony at bat. He knew how to be safely reckless and smashed out the first pitch for a hit. So it became Chuck Young's opportunity to win fame and possibly the ball game. Jim McNail's father gripped the plank he was sitting on with hands tighter than they held the plow. His whole being was in this game. Why was it so hard to swallow? Well, his own flesh and blood was down there, master-minding his pick-up team against the highly coached nine of the best school in that part of the country. Mr. McNail was glad that his wife had not come. The strain would have wounded her. It was impossible to remember that this was but a game. It wasn't. It was a trial of wills, of character, of all that Jim and his fellows had built into their lives.

Chuck's crack brought Jim's father out of his interior

debate. At first he didn't see the ball. Then several men and boys in the stands stood up, clutching with outstretched hands—a foul, after all. Still, Chuck had hit. Now he hit again, but too high, too high, if only the center fielder would kindly stumble—but no, he caught it, and Chuck walked dejectedly to the bench.

Rod Kregill, the mighty, took his stance, wiped one hand on a thigh and then the other. "*Strike*," called the umpire. Everson poured the second across the plate and Rod was a split-second late. "Strike two."

Jim's very thought was suspended in this crisis—the next moment vs. his future. Everything depended on the next pitch. If Rod could reach first, then he, Jim, would try to make the home run he had it in him to make, but—

The sound of wood on leather . . . Rod beating it toward first . . . the ball stopped by Everson . . . the straight, swift throw . . . the sound of ball in mitt . . . the sound of doom . . . a clear out, the score 3 to 3. Now if Tony could only hold them, they would have one more chance, since the two teams had prearranged to play out a tie.

Tony, on the mound, watched his support take their places. They were tired from the long strain as much as from the physical effort, worn down by the suspense and disappointment. Fatigue had got to Tony, too. He had held down Ironwood so that his mates could come to the edge of glory, and then they had failed to go beyond. This final half of the seventh brought back all the tension that Tony had felt before the game. He must hold them down. He must. But his fears of a misplay, one careless pitch, or faulty fielding invaded his spirit like a fog. He shook his head. The fog must not reach his eye.

Tony's first was too fast to cast a shadow; the batter struck at thin air. Tony counted twelve and a few more. He knew how to spoil a batter's timing. "Foul," he said to himself. The ball had curved like a cat's tail, right in to the batter's handle. Tony counted fifteen. The batter looked braced and wooden. That cheered Tony. He poured one in with that quick liquid motion of a perfectly executed throw. It had to follow his eye. It had to, and his eye was clear. The umpire called it a ball: too low. Tony counted and Jim signaled for more of the same. The batter failed to hit. One down, two more to go.

Ironwood's catcher was up. Tony remembered that he had nailed this guy with a low and inside pitch and gave him one. The batter flailed in vain. Tony counted only six and surprised Jim as well as the batter, who struck too quickly. One more pitch—and Tony sent it, special delivery. The batter boosted it, Jim caught it; two down and Ted Everson at bat.

Laurie was suffering. How could she hope that Ted would fail? *Ted* who had taken her for so many rides in that perfect car, who had danced with her until she knew where bliss was—on a dance floor in Ted's arms. Yet how could she wish Jim a broken heart? He cared for victory more than Ted could ever care.

Suddenly, Laurie sat up straighter, rigid with that clear discovery. *That* was the answer. Jim could *care* more than Ted. It was a revelation. Why hadn't she seen it before? Ted was wonderful and he did care for her. Jim was hardly what you called fun, but he was *life*, and Jim *more* than cared for her. She saw that in a blinding light. She was rooting for Jim in her mind, with all her heart, and no possible mistake.

Tony stood on the mound, alone, so alone it hurt—one against so many! He took a look at Jim's mitt. Jim was asking for Tony's prime pitch, the low and inside rocket. Tony threw. The sound of the bat was the crack of doom.

The ball shot out like something from a space platform, far beyond shortstop, far over the left fielder's head. Ted started to jog around the bases. The hundreds of Ironwood rooters jumped to their feet and were yelling, yelling, breaking through the ropes and out onto the field.

Laurie bowed her head. She could not bear to have anyone see her tears.

But someone did see. Headmaster Ironwood stooped over the girl and said, "I know how glad you feel, Laurie. Here's a dry handkerchief."

She shook her head. "May I . . . come . . . to see you . . . now? May I?"

"Why, certainly," replied the elderly man, who had supposed he had encountered all the surprises possible. "Come with me. But first we must congratulate Captain Ted."

"I'll wait," Laurie said. "Please."

19

The Winning Loss

THE SPECTATORS were edging their way out of the stands. Jim's eye caught the scoreboard's *Visitors* 3, *Ironwood* 4 without seeing. He did not need to see; those figures were burned indelibly in his heart and mind. He could not yet wholly realize that his year-long effort was over, that he had lost for good the slight hold on Ironwood School that he had planned.

Tony Wayland caught up with him and said, in an effort to lighten the blow, "A gun's quicker, but take a pitchfork to me if you like."

Jim started out of his daze. "You crazy? You pitched the best game of your life. Besides, I called for that pitch."

Frank Lafferty caught up with them. "Life does these things to you," he said to Jim. "You spend months building a barn. Then lightning strikes and it goes up in flames."

"We went up in one flame," Tony said.

"*Then,*" Frank continued slowly, "you collect the insurance."

Jim stared at his lifelong friend. "Too bad we weren't insured."

"In your case, the insurance is built in," Frank assured him. "Nobody lives as hard for an objective as you've lived without winning something."

"When do you leave us for the pulpit?" Tony asked with a wink at Jim—but an undertone of appreciation for the help.

"Good preaching's just facts—" Frank began, but by then the team had gathered around, all talking at once as they headed for the showers. Jim wrenched himself out of his depressed state to praise them on their playing.

Ted Everson met them at the door and said, "You fellows gave us the scare of the season. We've never played a sharper team, never played harder ourselves. But I'm here to tell you that the Sports Committee's serving tea in the gym in a few minutes. Get your showers and someone'll show you the way. They're also serving some pretty nifty girls, I might add."

The Burnsbrookers thanked him, shed their clothes, turned on the water of a dozen showers. Jim felt life reviving in him as the water rippled down his disciplined body, washing away the tension, the fatigue. The future took over as he toweled dry. He began to see the day in perspective: a defeat, but it had not killed him or any part of him. The central power in him glowed as strong as ever. He had been proven when tested in many of the ways that manhood is tested. A surge of masculinity ran through his veins. He looked at the team in various stages of dressing, talking again, vigorously revived. It was good to be one of such a company.

Jim was finishing dressing when a man approached him. He recognized Paul Atwood, the admissions dean who had shut him out of his promised land, but that was part of the past history which Jim was setting himself to forget. Dean Atwood was saying, "Our Headmaster, Mr. Ironwood, watched the game, McNail, and he invites you to have tea with Mrs. Ironwood and him at his home. I'll show you the way there, if you're ready."

"One shake, sir, the hair." When that was combed, Jim said, "Shall I leave my things here?"

Dean Atwood nodded and the two walked briskly to the Headmaster's house, where the dean left the boy. To Jim's surprise and delight, Laurie Anderson was sitting on the porch with Mrs. Ironwood and introduced Jim to the Headmaster's wife. She was a tall, kindly looking lady, with blue eyes that seemed to look into one's very being, offering welcome. Soon, she said to Laurie, "I thought that it would be pleasanter outdoors, in the garden, and so, if you will take our guest around back, I'll bring out the tea."

"You seem to be at home here," Jim said the moment Mrs. Ironwood vanished indoors, for he hoped to stave off any sympathy about the game.

Laurie sensed this and said, "That's the secret of this place, Jim. The Ironwoods do everything they can to make us all feel at home. It really is like a second home to me."

Jim wondered if she knew she was touching on his grief. But they had come out on a pleasant lawn, with an inviting-looking table, bearing tea-silver and frosted cake. Mr. Ironwood arrived from a side door with a teapot, his wife following, and somehow Jim felt eased into this company, as if he had known these people for years.

Laurie introduced Jim to the Headmaster, who said, "You and your boys gave us some highly uncomfortable moments this afternoon, Jim, but Mrs. Ironwood, at any rate, has forgiven you. She always expresses her moods in tea, and throws in a slice of cake, if she feels especially benevolent."

"What do the scones mean, then?" Laurie asked, smiling, "not to mention the buttered toast and jam?"

"You must be responsible for them," Mr. Ironwood said. "Symbols of pure affection." He turned back to Jim. "I have given orders to my staff to see to it that Miss Anderson's grades are kept so low that she will never graduate. We simply can't do without her."

"The staff seems to be obeying you, sir," Laurie said. "I got only a C in math."

"Good, good, and expect a D-minus on your next report."

Mrs. Ironwood broke in with, "When you two get tired of your fairy tales, we'll have tea." Then to Jim, she said, "You may not know it, but Miss Anderson is a steady inhabitant of our Honor Roll. Laurie, two lumps and no milk, I remember."

It was Jim's first experience with this sort of party, with two highly intellectual adults being as genial to him as the spring sunshine. Without being in the least embarrassing, Mrs. Ironwood somehow made him feel like a celebrity, and Laurie made him feel something else. This strange mixing of happy emotions, satisfaction and longing (a little) and wondering what next, lifted him above food, and he barely tasted the delicious sandwiches and the cake, nor counted his cups of tea. He was trying to reply to their questions while asking others in his mind: why was he here at this private party without his team? Why was Laurie here? Why did she look so beaming and laugh so easily? Because Ted Everson had won the game away from him? She must have known how desperately tragic the loss was to him. Why? Why?

Yet he could not dwell on these doubts, since both the Ironwoods kept inquiring about his life on the farm. Was the milking an irksome chore, especially in winter? What was the secret of raising such sweet-tasting strawberries, a box of which Laurie had given to them? And how had he and Tony Wayland ever gathered so adept a team?

Jim forgot his inner questions as he told about Frank Lafferty's mischance in his professional career, thus making it possible for Tony and himself to grow up in the baseball atmosphere.

Mr. Ironwood exclaimed, "There's compensation for you! Have you read Emerson's essay 'Compensation,' Jim?"

"No, sir, but I expect my sister has."

"I read that collection of profound truths aloud to the School every year, Jim. It's layman scripture. Does what you tell us mean that you are set on becoming a professional ballplayer? Or will you stick by Burnsbrook Farm?"

"No, sir. My brother Scott will do that. He's a born farmer. I like people too much to stick by the soil, though outdoors is my home. From what Uncle Frank has told me about pro baseball, I don't think I'd fit into that uncertain way of life very well, either."

Laurie broke in with, "Jim's too modest to tell about himself, Mr. Ironwood. He's a born worker with boys. My brother would follow him anywhere, just for the satisfaction of being ordered about by him. When Jim had to lay Dick off the team so that a better player could hold down right field, Dick took it without a word." Then Laurie put her napkin on the table. "I hate to leave, but there's first bell and I'm on work-crew. This has been a real privilege, Mrs. Ironwood. Thank you so much for inviting me."

"You know what *we* thank *you* for," Mrs. Ironwood said, and Jim wondered what that could possibly be. He and Mr. Ironwood rose, and Mrs. Ironwood left with Laurie.

Jim and the Headmaster sat down again and Mr. Ironwood said, "What Mrs. Ironwood was referring to just now was what that thoughtful girl has been telling us about you, Jim. This school administration has so many ramifications that I cannot keep informed on all the details. I pick the best managers I can find for each department and give each master his head. That is why I never heard of your wishing to enroll here as a day student last fall. Mr. Atwood was acting within the general framework which has firmed up through the years."

Jim's quick hope, which had glowed like a blow-upon spark, died away just as fast. Mr. Ironwood went on, "Laurie Anderson is a rare girl, which you may not need to be told. And she seems to consider you a rare specimen of the opposite sex."

"Beginning with Ted Everson," Jim blurted out, since Ted pervaded his thoughts.

"Yes," Mr. Ironwood concurred, "*beginning* with Ted, who is a promising young athlete. But not necessarily *ending* with him. I like to picture, for the students, each of us on his own particular conveyor-belt called *time*. Each of us proceeds at his own individual speed, which is the sum of all he thinks and does and deeply wishes to do. A girl may seem to glide along at the same rate as an engaging young fellow named Everson. But presently she finds herself pulling ahead and—of course, I may be mistaken about all this—and yet finds herself paralleling you. I do not pretend to read girls' minds, let alone hearts, but I must say that Laurie seems to have paid the most flattering attention to your career. She recited your long and varied efforts to produce a master team. And told how each of your efforts was followed by a setback. I won't say defeat, because you did not permit any setback to be a defeat.

"Now that, I must say, interested me. Laurie also explained how each of your refusals to be defeated brought a new and superior prospect to view. When she told me of your struggles upward I said to her, 'Do you know, we could use a young man with ability to survive defeat in such a way that it becomes a stepping stone to further advantage.' And when I said that her face brightened and she told me, 'That is Jim's ambition, to be connected with Ironwood School. All his life he has looked up to this School. He wanted to play ball with it, but couldn't, so he wanted to play against it, because even that is a sort of tie. But to work *for* Ironwood would be so wonderful that no words could express it.' Well, her eyes, her face, her voice expressed something very amiable, Jim, so I told her that I would see you after the game, in order that we might discuss the situation in a preparatory way."

Jim straightened in his chair. What was coming? Little electric thrills were starting in his mind and running out along his body. He said, "Once more, a loss has a lift in it, sir."

Mr. Ironwood replied, "When you have learned to look for the lift, as you call it, in a loss, you may have won something that even a victory can't give. I'm old-fashioned, Jim. I still read Robert Browning's poems and to my students I read his famous lines, 'Then welcome each rebuff that turns earth's smoothness rough . . .' It's in 'Rabbi Ben Ezra,' and you'll like it because you've already worked that part out for yourself.

"But I mustn't wander off the track, for you'll be wanting to take your team home soon. This is what I ask you to think about. Our sports department is large and one of the sports director's assistants is leaving us. If you wished to come in his place, we could take the matter up. But I must tell you that that job isn't good enough for you. It is static. It ends with itself.

"Now let me use my imagination. I can see you going to one of the colleges that prepares young men for responsible positions such as our sports director enjoys. If you spent the requisite number of years in college and then came to us to learn the ropes from our director, it is quite possible that you could qualify as a director in time. In fact, our director will reach the retirement age in a few years, and his job commands a very respectable salary and, of course, a house, in case the incumbent wishes to marry."

Jim could hardly talk for excitement, but the cost of such an education was almost prohibitive for him and he said so.

"Tomorrow morning, I am free to see you at ten o'clock and we can canvass that situation. There are many ways of self-help today for young men of integrity and real promise," Mr. Ironwood said.

"How can I thank you?" Jim exclaimed. "I'll be here at ten."

"Well, first the immediate thanks go to Laurie, but I suppose you would like to deliver them in person. And if you come here eventually and do a good job, that is thanks enough for me. Action is the gratitude that really matters."

Mr. Ironwood rose and Jim said, "I guess you'd like me to keep quiet about this."

"I hoped you'd suggest a certain amount of reticence," Mr. Ironwood replied with a smile. "Talking in advance of doing is a little like digging up your potatoes to see if they're growing. Tell your family, of course, and perhaps Laurie might like to hear, under conditions of secrecy."

Jim held out his hand. "I'll be seeing you at ten tomorrow morning, sir, and no words can tell you how much it would mean to me to become a part of Ironwood School."

"That's our chief entrance requirement," Mr. Ironwood assured him.

The two walked around to the front of the house. Jim ran up on the porch to thank his hostess, then started down the tree-lined lane that someday would be his—*his!*